The Mystery of the Engraved Letters and the Links

רזא דאתוון גליפין והשתלשלות

First Full English Translation BY

הרב מג בבל רז [HARAB MAG (The Chief Magician) of Mystery Babylon]

Acknowledgments

I would like to begin by acknowledging and blessing my spiritual twin brother YIRAH who is a very powerful holy Merovingian Magician like myself. He did all the backcover for this book! I am so grateful to him for this! Also special thanks to his chief disciple Scott who did the front cover!

I would also like to acknowledge and bless my chief disciple Yaqob who helped me review this entire work.

יהוה bless both of you greatly bshem HaMashiah Yisrael!

Table of Contents:

Mystery of the Engraved Letters…………..pg 13

Tosefta: Shabbathian Commentary to Sifra Detziniutha……………………………….pg 61

Annotations to Tosefta…………………..pg 77

Hebrew/Aramaic Text………………...pg 79

Exordium From The Translator

"The Mystery of the Engraved Letters' is an extremely advanced esoteric Qabbalistic text. It is paired and studied alongside 'TZADDIQ YESOD OLAM'. Like 'TZADDIQ YESOD OLAM', this text is a very advanced esoteric Shabbathian text. The easy proof is the discussion of the 2 Great Secret Lights, a very esoteric doctrine revealed by our holy exalted prophet Nathan of Gaza. And so the keys of 'TZADDIQ YESOD OLAM' are all given here.

The book has a large focus on the esoteric mystical properties of our divine seals, thus aiding the Holy Magician. But it is also a very advanced esoteric and technical revelation of Maaseh Breyshith and the beginning of the highly technical and complex system of the Lurianic Qabbalah. Without proper full initiation into the entire Lurianic Qabbalah, I'm afraid to state that this book will not at all be fully comprehended! Nevertheless, I have translated it in order that for those who read it, that they may glean whatever they may glean.

Finally, I have a added an addendum at the end of the book. It is a small translated section of a very critical principal Shabbathian text for the purposes of helping to elucidate certain complex technical sections in this book.

General Introduction

It is known that every point is in the mystery of 3. End, middle, and beginning in the mystery of Upper Waters, Lower Waters, and Middle Waters. To understand the matter, a parable is necessary because:

"...from the phallus/flesh I see ALWAH (The Goddess)." ~ Sefer Iyob 19:26

Know that the matter is over Thought and HOKHMAH and Will. By way of the parable: from the beginning it falls to man his thought. And afterwards, he becomes wise if he brings this thought to operation/actualization. If not and even if this thought goes out to operation/actualization with some matter it will be; this thought will be until a thought that is more correct nears him. And afterwards he considers the correct path. And my strength has strong agreement to bring this matter to actualization. And you will find here 3 levels in Thought. And it is Thought, HOKHMAH, and Will. And these 3 are in the brain because the First Thought is called the First Thought. And it is the Thought of the Primordial One of all Primordials. And the second level is HOKHMAH of Thought that is called Primordial Sealed Thought. And the

3rd level is Will of Thought. And from Thought comes Potential. And from Potential, Actualization. And just as there exists 3 levels – Thought, HOKHMAH, and Will in potential. And so there exists in actualization in the same way. And so Thought which is in great concealment goes to potentiality and from potentiality to actualization. And then the actualization is recognized by everything. And from the midst of the actualization is recognized the potential of the actualization. His Thought and Will are good; until here is the parable. If you understand this parable you will see concerning this parable the matter of the 10 Sfiroth – [Kether Hokhmah Binah] – [Hesed Geburah Tifereth] - [Netzah Hod Yesod Malkuth]. Kether Hokhmah Binah are the mystery of the Thought of the Primordial One to all Primordials. Primordial Thought, Will, and Thought; these 3 are the mystery of Thought. Hesed, Geburah, and Tifereth are the mystery of Thought. HOKHMAH and Will are potential. And Netzah, Hod, and Yesod are the mystery of [Thought, HOKHMAH, Thought] actualization. And MALKHUTH is complete actualization in the mystery of the crownlet in the mystery of KETHER – the end of an action is the beginning of thought.

Know because the holy Name יהוה – יה is the mystery of KETHER HOKHMAH BINAH – the concealed aeon/emanation. And the letters וה are the mystery of the revealed aeon/emanation. And it is the mystery of the Son and Daughter. Even though we said that HESED GEBURAH TIFERETH are potentiality, with respect to actuality it is NETZAH HOD YESOD MALKHUTH. But with respect to the concealed aeon it is called HESED GEBURAH TIFERETH, the principle of actualization. And afterwards, it was said that KETHER HOKHMAH BINAH are Thought, HOKHMAH, and Will of Thought. And the letter ו is called TIFERETH which is called the Son. And the principal of Thought is HOKHMAH. And actualized Will is the letter ו. It is BINAH [of] HESED GEBURAH TIFERETH even though BINAH is the Will with respect to Thought in order to arrange actualization. She is the Thought of the Primordial One to all Primordials. HESED is HOKHMAH of Thought, GEBURAH is the Will of Thought. And everything is to arrange actualization and TIFERETH is the Actualizer/actualized. And BINAH [of] HESED GEBURAH which are Thought, HOKHMAH, and Will to actualize the letter ו. They are to the letter ה the mystery of the Daughter with respect to Thought, HOKHMAH, and Will of Thought. The letter ה: BINAH is from the Primordial One to all Primordials of the Thought of the letter ה. HESED is Primordial Sealed Thought of the letter ה.

GEBURAH is the Will of the letter ה. And the 3 of Thought are the letter ה. And TIFERETH, NETZAH, and YESOD are Thought, HOKHMAH, and Will of the actualized letter ה. And the letter ה is actualization. And NETZAH and HOD are considered as 1 because it is known that the essence of the grasping of judgments is the mystery of its Externalities. And it is the mystery of the evil Externalities. And already it is known that each Sfirah contains 10 Sfiroth until EYN SOF and Eyn Takhlith. And all we have written is the general path to Thought, HOKHMAH, and Will of Thought, the letter ו, the actualization of the letter ו, thought of letter ה, and the actualization of the letter ה. You form thyself in KETHER and likewise in HOKHMAH, BINAH, and all the Sfiroth. And do not be perplexed as to why BINAH is the mystery of Will to Thought. The letter ו and Thought of the Primordial One to all Primordials are to actualize the letter ו. And this ה in GEBURAH is the Will to Thought. And TIFERETH is the Thought of the Primordial One to all Primordials to actualize. Accordingly, BINAH is the mystery of the Will which did not spread with HOKHMAH. And from there She receives and bestows the shefa to the extremities. Therefore, with respect to Thought She is the Will. And with respect to actualization She is the Thought of the Primordial One to all Primordials.

But the letter ה was concealed in the essences of The Blessed One (EYN SOF) when He went out to Thought and actualization from the extremities so to speak. And do not consider GEBURAH twice except once because BINAH is considered actualized from the Primordial One to all Primordials. The essence of the intention is to unify Lower SHEKHINAH with Upper SHEKHINAH – the end of an act [MALKHUTH] is the beginning of Thought [BINAH].

Also, know because what we have said that the grasping of the judgments are in HOD. And it was not the intention God forbid in all universes/aeons because in truth from BINAH is aroused judgments, the mystery of preserved wine. And GEBURAH is the mystery of revealed wine. And HOD is the mystery of fermented wine. And it is the mystery of leaven and the evil inclination, the Thought of the Externalities. But this does not exist in all the Universes God forbid. And you will understand this because in truth all of the Merkabah is the holy Name of the 4 Universes Atziluth, Briah, Yetzirah, and Assiyah. And the 4 Universes are the mystery of יהוה. And afterwards, the general path is the Universe of Atziluth even though its particulars are divided into 10 until EYN SOF and Eyn Takhlith. From every place the general path of the entire Universe of Atziluth is the mystery of י, the mystery of Thought at the end/tip. And HOKHMAH is the body of יוד. And the Universe of Briah in its principle/inclusion is the mystery of Will and the mystery of Upper ה. And in BINAH are the tittles/ends/extremities of GEDULLAH and GEBURAH. The explanation is that BINAH includes the hesedim and the geburoth. And the entire Universe of Yetzirah is in its principle/inclusion the mystery of ו. The mystery of TIFERETH includes HESED and GEBURAH. And in it dwells TIFERETH of Atziluth. And it is TIFERETH of HOKHMAH because so is the general path of all of Atziluth. And it is the mystery of יוד which is HOKHMAH like was mentioned above. And the entire Universe of Assiyah and its principle/inclusion is the mystery of MALKHUTH, the mystery of last ה. If so, when we divide the 10 Sfiroth of the general path of the Universes/Aeons, then the Sfiroth of NETZAH, HOD, YESOD, and MALKHUTH begin from Yetzirah of Yetzirah. If so, even Briah of Yetzirah does not have grasping except sometimes by way of rising/removing, God forbid, the light that dwells in TIFERETH which is ו of Yetzirah in the mystery of the concealment of the faces when it is written:

"I will surely hide…" ~ Sefer Debarim 31:18

In the rising/removal of the eyes which is the light of HOKHMAH. And then, God forbid, the judgments strengthen until their root in Briah. And sometimes until the ground of Atziluth. But from there and above they do not reach. And there exists in this a great mystery. And it is explained in the mystery of the letters. What is the matter? The Accuser is over the potential/power of 4 colors. And he was purified from them. And this was not perceived. And already until now, Briah is the mystery of potentiality but it is not Atziluth which is the mystery of Thought. Accordingly, HaQlippoth do not have a head. And when we do the will the of Eternal, then we bring down the Thoughtful Light so to speak. And the judgments are purified and sweetened and they are rejected from rejection until rejection until the Universe is purified in its entirety and there does not remain any judgments except on the lowest level which is the mystery of the lowest [realms].

BEGINNING

It is known from our holy Torah that was given with 22 letters and the final 5, that they are purified and refined 7 times[1]. And it is necessary to know that the holy letters are not in agreement according to the letters of the nations where it is not found in their writing one reason for the essence or attribute of a letter. But the letters of our Torah, each and every letter hints at its essence/attribute to many Universes without end. And there is no end to state them, it is impossible. And to clarify them we do not have the power except to speak over each and every letter the general path of what is the root and over some Universe hinted in its attribute/property. And we begin with the letter א.

The mystery of the letter א:

We find in the explanations of this א HaQadosh Barukh Hu. And He is the 1st and the last. According to the Name, א is the head of the letters. Therefore, HaQadosh Barukh Hu is the Head to everything. It was said how HaQadosh Barukh Hu

---

[1] C.F. Sefer Tehillim 12:6

was hinted at in the properties of א. Is it not written:

"...for ye saw no manner of image..." ~ Sefer Debarim 4:15

"To whom will you liken EL?..." ~ Sefer Yeshayahu 40:18?

But it is necessary you understand that before HaQadosh Barukh Hu created His Universe, His Name was concealed in Himself. And everything was concealed in His essence. And the 4 Universes correspond to the 4 letters of יהוה Blessed is He. And they were concealed in His essence until they were not perceived. And it was impossible for Him to form them in His essence except in the mystery of concealed roots. And every Universe was taller than its companion. And likewise, its root was taller than its companion. Just as it is impossible to speak except the ear is broken, it was spoken in them the mystery of 4 concealed colors in His essence. And from their power HaQadosh Barukh Hu created the 4 Universes and HQBH dwelled over them and below them and between them, even after the 4 Universes went out. And all the more so at the time of their concealment, they were not yet perceived at all. And they were concealed in His midst. And we know that corporeal man was apportioned a torso which is his middle. Without the torso are 4 levels. The 1st level: the neck with the hands. The 2nd level: the level of the heart (another time I heard: the 2nd level is until the navel. The 3rd level is from the navel until the phallus and the principle of the 4th level is the feet.). The 3rd level: the portion of the belly and the bowels. The 4th level: the thighs with the phallus. Likewise it is necessary to understand, to break the ear, the 4 Universes that HQBH created, so to speak, in His midst. And HATHOKH[2] was divided into the 4 levels of the 4 Universes. And He was so to speak over them, in their head and end until without end. How it is known that HATHOKH of His essence is the attribute of the letter ו and it is extended. And if so, it was said that before HQBH created the Universes, they were concealed in His essence the 4 colors what was now the middle. And it hints at the property of ו. And it was from before He was concealed in His essence. This is hinted at the letter א with its property; the property of the letter א is: י above, ו below, and י in the middle. י above hints at HQBH creating all the Universes until no end. And the י below hints at HQBH who is the end of all the Universes until EYN SOF. And the letter ו in the middle hints at the middle and it was concealed in His essence.

---

[2] התוך (HATHOKH) signifies middle/interior – codeword for TIFERETH.

His Name was concealed in Him with the mystery of the 4 concealed colors that are called the roots of the Name יהוה. The roots of the roots are the 4 Universes[3].

When it arose in His uniform Will to create the Universe to make known his Divinity. For there is no king without people and no lord without slaves. According to the greatness of the lord, through its value, a slave is subdued. And whatever slave is perceived more greater, the dominion of his lord is subdued before his lords. For this reason, it arose in His Will that 4 concealed colors go out like the boundary of the 4 Universes until it came to a thick and coarse corporeal boundary in order to create man on a low level in order that he would see his lowness and the greatness of his Lord and the Master of his dominion and the work of his hands like it says:

"For I see thy heavens…" ~ Sefer Tehillim 8:3

In order that man is subdued before HQBH and serves his Creator with fear and trembling. And for this reason it arose in the Will of HQBH that they

---

[3] Annotation of the scribe: "If it is difficult to thee why the middle are 4 levels and hints at the property of the letter ו which is the number 6, and why it is not appropriate for there to be 6 Universes corresponding to the 6 levels; know that the truth is that the 6 levels are the mystery of the 6 sides. But it is prohibited to ask what is above and below. And everything will be explained at length." C.F. Talmud Babli Tractate Hagigah 11B.

go out and come to the boundary of the 4 Universes. And He did not give them existence in its midst so to speak for the reason mentioned above. For will the hand of יהוה certainly be shortened[4]? But it will be the way of a parable of the lord with his slaves in one boundary in one chamber. The greatness of lord is not known from the greatness of the slave. But the slave needs to be outside the partition of the lord. Likewise, it was necessary for the 4 Universes to go out the boundary. And when it arose in His Will, the GOOD was before EYN SOF - pleasure and desire. And the way of a parable in man – the will arouses in the brain the potential of the action that is born. For seed comes from the brain so to speak to break the ear. The head of א we call the Upper Light. And from it was aroused one spark. And it descended to the midst of the middle of the א. And this spark actualized the mystery of engraving/letter in HATHOKH of EYN SOF. When it comes to the boundary of the 4 Universes it engraves from the concealed roots the root of the Name יהוה that was concealed. And the Name comes to actualization. And it actualized another engraving/letter in the middle to build within it another which will engrave the supreme Light of the boundary of the Universes, each Universe over

---

[4] C.F. Sefer Bamidbar 11:23

its foundation. The beginning was spoken from the Holy Name which comes from the concealed root to potential and actualization. And with our words will be understood the properties of the letters until the letter ׳ which is the first letter of the Holy Name. And afterwards, we spoke about the 4 Universes which went out to the boundary via actualization of the Holy Name in the potential/power of the Upper Light.

Know that the spark descended to HATHOKH inside the Heart[5] – the concealed root from the Universe of Briah which is the root of the 2nd level. If it was descending to the concealed root from Atziluth which is the root of the 1st level, it was returning to its root, therefore it descended to the 2nd level. And the 1st level prevented it from returning to its root from the power of ignition and knocking it down. And it was impossible for it to descend to the 3rd or 4 level because they did not have power to endure it. But in the 2nd level, even so, there was ignition from the power of the Light of the great and awesome spark. From every place it has a little standing so to speak to come to actualization when the heart is a little like the brain as is known. And from the power of ignition there will be actualization. From this power it came to the engraving/letter like it was explained.

---

[5] Codeword for TIFERETH.

The mystery of the letter ב:

Behold, the descent of the spark is the mystery of the letter ב. The going out of the spark – in breaking the ear you need to form in thy intelligence an opening of a portal to bring it out. And if you write the point of the head of the א and form the opening of a portal is forms the letter ב.

For this reason, HaTorah begins with the letter ב. The commandments begin with א. If HaTorah began with:

"I am יהוה thy Alohim…" ~ Sefer Shmoth 20:2

Over who would the [1st] commandment fallen? But HaTorah began with ב which was the beginning of בריאה (BRIAH) which He created to make Himself known. And so then the commandment *"I am יהוה thy Alohim"* would have fallen to ב.

The mystery of the letter ג:

It is necessary you know that when the spark descended to HATHOKH inside the heart, from it sparkled 2 sparks. And incline thy ear to the parable – if an ember falls burning over matter, from it sparkle sparks to the sides and the body does not decrease. Likewise, so to speak, from the spark sparkled 2 points which with respect to the great spark are called 2 sparks. 2 points – 1 to the left and 1 to the right. And they are the mystery of the roots of KETHER HOKHMAH BINAH.

And they were considered as 1 as is known. And they are in the mystery of the concealed point in His essence. And it is the mystery of the letter ג like this:

ג

The head is the great spark. And the two feet of the letter are the 2 points which spread from it. And it is the mystery of KETHER HOKHMAH BINAH which are considered as 1. And do not imagine any letter, measure, or border God forbid except the root of the roots.

And when the spark spread with the points inside the heart, in its midst was a great ignition. Accordingly, the light of the spark is the light of the brain. And it was greater and it was aroused inside the heart to request power to endure. And from the power of the arousal of HATHOKH was aroused the spark to rise above. It thought that the power came to it to return above. And the spark with the points were aroused. But in truth, it was not possible for it to rise like mentioned above [for the Universe of Atziluth restricted it from rising]. And the Will of the Creator EYN SOF was for the spark to think it could rise in order that through its arousal the 2 points would be aroused to collide this with that. And from the power of their collision, from them would go out, with the power of the upper spark, another spark. And this 2nd spark would sparkle many sparks without number and end. And if you desire to ask why from the spark sparkled 2 points and from the 2nd spark sparkled many sparks? You need to understand that the upper spark descended softly and so it sparkled 2 sparks. But the 2nd spark, from the power of the arousal of the spark, the points arose and were aroused. From the power of collision, colliding this with that, from them went out a spark in the mystery of a shooting arrow. Because they sparkled many sparks without measure and end.

The mystery of the letter ד:

And behold, this second spark is the mystery of the letter ד because the 2nd spark went out from the collision of the points. And their arousal from the arousal of the upper spark. And if so, the upper spark with the points were in the mystery of the letter ג. Now, from the power of their arousal they had conjugal union together – the spreading of the spark between the points. From them was made the horizontal line of the letter like this: ¯ . And afterwards, the 2nd spark spread and the spreading was from the aspect of the Right. And it is the feet of ד and the vertical line. And it became the letters ד, ה, and ו. They are from the Holy Name. And they will be explained in their place – afterwards, the letter י which is the 1st letter of the Name.

The mystery of the letter ט, ה,ז:

And now will be explained the letter ז. And it is necessary to know that when the ignition began in the heart, heat was created so to speak. And they developed so to speak the power of all HATHOKH which were requesting a reason to strengthen corresponding to the upper spark to return it to its place. They strengthened all their power to the inside of the heart to pressure the light to rise but in truth it was impossible for them to act as mentioned above. And this was the will of the Creator that all the colors be aroused. And from this power/potential was aroused the spark with the points. And with the 1st spark, many sparks sparkled. And through their arousal was made from them the mystery of aggregation like a flame to be like one spark. And afterwards, power spread to the upper spark in the mystery of the neshamah. Because many sparks were gathered in the mystery of rubbing/spreading. And the power of the upper spark is in the mystery of the neshamah so to speak. And from the power, they aroused HATHOKH. And they strengthened all their power. This was the action – the Supreme Power of HATHOKH drew and took the upper spark in the midst of the sparks. And now it began to draw forth from HATHOKH this letter and engraving. And when it began to draw forth and engrave, now was born the power of Thought to draw forth and engrave all the power/potential of the colors until He drew forth and engraved all the roots of the Name יהוה Blessed is He. And the roots came to potential/power and actualization. And if all the eyes of thee see, perceive, and understand the verse:

"…through my phallus I see ALWAH (The Holy Goddess)." ~ Sefer Iyob 19:26

In the beginning, the spark descended and rested in the midst of HATHOKH of the heart. And Will and Power/Potential are that which gives birth. And afterwards, from the power of the ignition of the heart sparkled many sparks in the mystery of a shooting arrow. And afterwards, it became in the mystery of aggregation, the mystery of spreading/rubbing. And afterwards, it spread in them the power of the neshamah, the power of the spark. And from the power of the power of the neshamah was born the mystery of Thought as is known. The neshamah is the mystery of Thought. And this is the Thought of the Primordial One to all Primordials which was the thought to engrave the roots of יהוי. And from the midst of the concealed colors, they came to potential and actualization. And afterwards, Primordial Sealed Thought spoke – after Thought of the Primordial One to all Primordials was actualized. The roots of יהוה came to potential/power and actualization. And the power of Primordial Thought was born. And it is primordial to all actualizations. The Holy Name actualized the structure of the Universes which will be explained with help of HASHEM.

And now will be understood the properties of the letters זחט. From what many sparks gathered in 1 spark – the head of the letter ז. In it was born the mystery of Thought. And it is to it the mystery of existence and standing. And it is the mystery of the feet and pillar of ז. And the neshamah which spread in it with Thought divided the feet of ז into 2. And when you divide the feet of ז into 2 portions with the length, it became from the letter ז the letter ח. For Thought enclothes the neshamah, and the neshamah is the internality of Thought. And when it was possible for Thought to endure the power of the neshamah, the feet of ח drew to each other. And they fused in the mystery of the 5 levels of the neshamah. And the roof above over the ח was divided a little in order for the neshamah to have an opening to its root and it will be possible for it to endure it. And afterwards, the letter ח became the letter ט as mentioned above.

The mystery of the letter ו, ה, י:

Now we will begin to explain the properties of the letter י. And we will explain all 4 letters of the Holy Name. And why ה is doubled in it. And you will find rest in thy soul. And we return to the matter mentioned above to the mystery of Thought of the Primordial One to all Primordials which was the thought to engrave the roots of יהוה from the midst of the 4 concealed colors which came to power and actualization. And behold, it thought to request a reason to strengthen HATHOKH and progress its power in order that through this, its supreme Light would engrave and draw forth more and more. The Thought of the Primordial One to all Primordials concealed the light of the great spark with the sparks mentioned above in the mystery of concealment until the erection of the light in the mystery of the apex/tip of י. And the intention of the concealment – that HATHOKH would think that already the light returned above. And they considered it well what they did wherewith at the beginning they strengthened until it returned from the light and above until there did not remain except like the apex/tip of the י. From this power, they returned to arouse their power to HATHOKH of the heart and to strengthen the power in order to return everything above to be like they were. And HATHOKH did not perceive in the mystery of concealment. Accordingly, HATHOKH is the Thoughtless Light[6] – just a simple[7] Light. And He intended that HATHOKH strengthen as mentioned above. Suddenly, the light spread more from what it was. The Light drew

---

[6] According to the holy prophet Nathan of Gaza, the essence of the Thoughtless Light is the Straight Line.
[7] Here is implied 'stupidity', the Light being Thoughtless. C.F. the mystical saying: 'The Qlippoth have no head'.

forth and engraved the power that strengthened corresponding to the midst of its light so to speak. At the beginning, the light was found concealed in the mystery of apex/tip of י. Afterwards, it spread in the mystery of HATHOKH of the י. And when it was concealed, the concealed light actualized in order that it spread more. And afterwards, therefore, the apex/tip is in the mystery of KETHER. And HATHOKH of י is in the mystery of HOKHMAH because had it not been for the tip/apex, there would not have been spreading. Afterwards, HATHOKH of י descended. From it was an exceedingly tall Light in the mystery of the lower tip/apex of י which was concealed likewise. The Light was brought down below in the mystery of the apex/tip but not for the reason mentioned above. Above we said that the reason was that HATHOKH would think that the Light returned above. But now, they already thought like mentioned above. And it did not occur to them that it was just concealed in the lower tip/apex. HATHOKH thought that they were annulled according to a measured value that they were able to endure. And He returned to them their power which they lost. And He intended that they strengthen to request their power from the lower tip/apex. The Light spread more. The Light, the upper tip, HATHOKH/middle, and the lower tip became a complete י. And therefore י is 1 point and the number 10. Accordingly, before they spread to make the complete י, they were in the mystery of 3 lines. And every line had a head, middle, and end – behold 9! And afterwards, they spread this with that in the mystery of complete י as mentioned above. Behold 10! For this is a great principle – the entire spreading which spread the Light left the reshimu[8] from the Highest in its place. And it was found that the Light began to stand with the property of the letter י which is smallest among the letters. From this power HATHOKH thought to strengthen corresponding to the small letter like was explained. In order that it will complete the actualization of the engraving/letter and draw forth the concealed roots from the power of collision[9].

After the Light stood according to the property of י as mentioned above, the power/potential of the concealed roots began to probe a side that was possible for them to touch the great Light in order to return to themselves the power they lost from them. And they strengthened their power in

---

[8] Residual Light.
[9] The Straight Line is the Builder of the Universes, which in essence is the Thoughtless Light. What is being described here is a complex deceptive strategy on the part of Eyn Sof. The Thoughtless Light seeks to return Itself and everything to back to its source. But Eyn Sof needs the opposite to happen to create and spread the Universes. Ergo, the complex deceptive strategy. The Thoughtless Light is deceived into thinking it can rise back to its source, but is blocked on its partial ascent, and then recoils back more, thus executing the Will of Eyn Sof in spreading the Light.

HATHOKH of the י. And they made the י encircle over them. And their power stood in the midst of the encircling in the mystery of the embrace of male and female. For HATHOKH is the mystery of the female since HATHOKH gave birth and encircled י which is the mystery of the male. And the Light did not spread to draw forth the power. And they thought is was good for they found themselves standing in the midst of the י. They thought they could overpower the Light of י and return to themselves the power they lost and be more strengthened to overpower. And they drew forth the encircling line to straighten it. And their power stood in the midst of the encircling. And they stood over the Line in order to overpower it. And when they stood, so the light of the spark spread and strengthened over/against their power. And the power drew forth to the midst of the Light of the Line. And it sweetened their power in the midst of the line of י. And you will find now that in the beginning, they made the line over them to encircle. And their power stood in the midst of the Line which became the letter of the first ה from the Name. And She was in the mystery of the embracing of male and female. And therefore, the 1st ה is the mystery of the Upper Mother in the mystery of BINAH. In any case, they began to probe their aspects. And whatever they erected afterwards is the power over the Line which is the mystery of ו. And accordingly, there their power was sweetened to the midst of the Line. Therefore, the letter ו from the Holy Name sweetens everything. And it tempers everything. And it is the Measuring Line. And when it also did not occur to them that they had contact in the mystery of the embracing of male and female, their attribute was lost. They were no longer considered strong and it was also impossible for them to strengthen anymore because already they were sweetened by HATHOKH ו – the all supreme of the roots. And they were only considered as they were in the beginning in the mystery of embracing. And they returned to have the letter ו encircle over them. And this is the last letter ה of the Name יהוה. And there, they have grasping. And you will find that the letters of יהוה Blessed is He came to power/potential when already all the power/potential of the concealed roots descended with the power of the upper spark. And if you desire to ask why the last ה remained and not the first ה? It is necessary for you to know that the letters יה are in the mystery of 'loves who never separate'[10]. And there is conjugal union without cessation. And it was not possible for them to endure the Light. The reason is that there it is without cessation because there the male is with

---

[10] C.F. Sefer HaZohar 3:4A

the attribute of י. And it is a small letter so to speak without ceasing. Therefore, it returned and became וה from יה. And now the mystery of the male is ו which is longer hinting over the Measuring Line. And it ceased to give measurement when it was possible to endure. And now the Thought of the Primordial One to all Primordials was completed. Already it drew forth the power of the roots of יהוה. And afterwards, the Holy Name came to actualize the letters of יהוה exactly. And do not think of any image of a letter God forbid!!! Except we clarified now the power of the concealed roots which became so to speak 1 Light and spark like the neshamah to them. And from now on, the GOOD was able to actualize according to His Will. And now all the lights spread which we mentioned in the midst of the Light of יהוה. And there remained the mystery of the reshimu above.

And now we have spoken from Thought of the Primordial One to all Primordials. The actualizations that The Holy Name actualized were in order to create the Universes. They came to the boundary like it arose in the Will of the Creator. Like we recalled at the beginning of the words. And he considered that the power of colors not be mixed with what remained – the dross. For the best/supreme was purified and is the power of their right. And the power of their left remained even though if was impossible to say that this is the right and that is the left. But it is well, after the breaking, that you may say left and right. It was said by request here of the Supreme Power and it is the power of their right. And He considered that the dross not be mixed with the purified light so to speak. And the reshimu mentioned revolved around all the lights revolving around EYN SOF like a wall dividing between the purified light and the light that remained. And the reshimu is from a taller light that revolves closer to it. For example, it is more near to the reshimu than the spark of the light of the upper point. And afterwards, the reshimu is from the 1st point. And afterwards, from the 2nd point. And afterwards, from the 4th point. And afterwards, from the neshamah of all neshamoth. And afterwards, from the Thought of the Primordial One to all Primordials. And afterwards, from the tip/apex of י. And afterwards from HATHOKH of י. And afterwards, from the lower tip/apex. And afterwards, from the complete י. And afterwards from the body of ה. And afterwards from the point of ה. And afterwards from the body of ו, from the head of ו, from the body of the point of ה. And afterwards, from Primordial Thought. And afterwards, from יהוה which went out to actualization: from י, from, from ה, from ו, and from last ה which encircles the externality, and there they have grasping. And the upper spark concealed itself in the reshimu mentioned above – in the midst of the interior of the Heart. And the reshimu revolved around EYN SOF. It was not perceived by them – 'neither white, black, green, or red and no color at all'[11]. And the Light of יהוה was concealed in their midst. It illuminated the end of illumination until it was perceived in them. For example, if a man takes a bright polished mirror and takes it hither and thither, it is impossible for him to perceive its light. But if he gives it standing and proper placement, it is possible for him to enjoy its light. Likewise, so to speak, from the power of ignition and collision, they were not [able] so to speak to illuminate existence and it was not possible for them to perceive. And now, His great Light was perceived in the midst of the reshimu. Accordingly, it came to the principle of existence and understand.

And behold, in order for the actualization of the Universes to begin, they had to be able to endure. The Circle was broken to 2^{12}. And this is the mystery of: 'it broke and did not break'[13] which is

---

[11] C.F. Sefer HaZohar 1:15A

[12] C.F. Sefer HaZohar 2:180A. Also C.F. RAMAQ's commentary to Zohar 1:15B in his Sefer Or Yaqar and many other citations in the principal Lurianic, Shabbathian, & Frankist texts such as Sefer Emeq HaMalakh and Shaarey Gan Eden & etc.

[13] See note 10.

stated in HaZohar. And the breaking is the mystery of birth. The inner Light went outside to sparkle colors. The internality was engraved from the midst of the externality. And to break the ear, you will understand from the birth of chicklet – from the midst of the internality of the egg. And the chicklet is engraved from the midst of the internality and breaks the egg to 2. And know that all the Light of the Circle did not go out from the externality except half and a second half. It was said there in the mystery of the concealed Light – the Light of יהוה went – all of it to the midst of the externality except there remained the reshimu from EYN SOF in the midst of the 2nd half. It was said: and from the reshimu in the midst of the circles, He took the Light of יהוה with Him of the Right and the Left half remained there. Before the breaking, there did not exist relevance to say Right or Left. In any case, it is possible to say so like we wrote above that is according to the Supreme Power. And the reason it remained in the midst of the external colors of the Left half: 1: in order that the Light would come to endure the concealment so to speak from its Light. And it is the concealed Light. And furthermore, because all the Light of the reshimu was going from the outside to the external colors which were not existing at all. And the principle: and it was inevitable that they would run after their internal Light and it would return

God forbid to what it was like before. Therefore, half of the reshimu remained. And also the reshimu from the Light of יהוה Blessed Be He remained. And they were not perceived as much as the going out of the Light until they saw the Universes the Creator built with this internal Light of the Right that went out from them. And afterwards, they began to run but the Creator had already acted. They were not able to return to like it was before except they found themselves grasping in a broken place as is known.

And when half of the reshimu of the Right went from the midst of the external colors and went with it, the Light of יהוה and the Right half spread at the end of the spreading And the Light of יהוה went from the midst of the internal reshimu to stand over them. And then the Light of the reshimu of the Right half spread to EYN SOF and to EYN TAKHLITH[14]. For this reason, the Light of יהוה Blessed is He went to stand so to speak over the reshimu. He certainly supports His roots resting in Eden. And so to speak He received from His roots to spread the Light to EYN SOF and EYN TAKHLITH. And He is the Light we find in the words of the ancients. And He is at the end of the Garment that covers everything. And therefore, the

---

[14] EYN SOF is Upper EYN SOF. EYN TAKHLITH can be thought of as Lower EYN SOF.

attribute of TIFERETH of Atziluth is in the mystery of EYN SOF. Accordingly, He covers all HaSfiroth as is known. And the reason that the Light of יהוה went over the reshimu is for 2 reasons. We wrote above that He ceased in order that it will be possible to endure the Light in the midst of reshimu. So that it would be possible to come there to the corporeal boundary. And furthermore, the external colors thought that the supreme Light returned to its roots to be like it was before and afterwards, the half of the reshimu would not exist so that greater power go out from them than the [other] half which remained to them. And they did not run after the Right half. But in truth, it did not return to its roots completely except over the reshimu. On the contrary, this was the action the Universes understood after the tzimtzum[15] of the lights so to speak. And the light remaining in tzimtzum would become ADAM QADMON to all QADOMIM as is known. And it was as if the Light of יהוה remained in the midst of the reshimu. And it was not able to endure in the mystery of:

"...adam cannot see me and live." ~ Sefer Shmoth 33:20

---

[15] "The Breaking" is before the 1st tzimtzum.

Therefore, its Light was concealed above over them but it did not return completely to its roots. Accordingly, it already came to the principle of יהוה Blessed is He.

And after the Light of the reshimu spread to EYN SOF and EYN TAKHLITH as mentioned above, it became the mystery of movement – the mystery of tzimtzum in the midst of the reshimu until in their midst was seen a vacuous cavity. And it was not entirely vacuous God forbid there remained the Light relative to its endurance. And it is the Light of ADAM QADMON which we have mentioned. Through Him the Universes came to actualization through the power of the Will of the Highest Creator. And now it was said to break the ear, the roots of the roots of the 10 Sfiroth. And do not think any attribute or limit God forbid. The upper light is in the mystery of KETHER over the Light of יהוה Blessed is He. And the Light of יהוה Blessed is He is in the mystery of HOKHMAH in the mystery of the Head to all the Universes. And He is QADMON to every matter and the internal colors of the Right – the reshimu that we have mentioned. They are in the mystery of the Mother in the mystery of the pleasure/delight of יהוה. And they are in the mystery of BINAH and in the mystery of the Upper Point. And the Light of the Blessed One which spread from יהוה EYN SOF to the midst of the reshimu until it spread to EYN SOF and EYN TAKHLITH. And they covered this Light of EYN SOF which is in the mystery of TIFERETH and the reason we mentioned above. And the Light that remained in the midst of the tzimtzum is the mystery of ADAM QADMON. And it is with respect to HAQADMON and with respect to YESOD. And therefore we call Him ADAM QADMON. There ADAM fell over YESOD which is Lower ADAM who is YESOD of the Universe of Assiyah as it is written:

"...tzaddiq yesod olam." ~ Proverbs 10:25

Accordingly, He is so to speak YESOD of HaQadosh Barukh Hu. Therefore, He is called ADAM QADMON because HQBH is called QADMON. And whatever the Light strengthened encircled the cavity which is in the mystery of the Crown over YESOD. And take this principle in thy hand what we have said above that before the breaking, in the beginning the Light was spreading in the midst of the interior of the Heart in potential/power in the mystery of engraving. And now, after the breaking, everything became actualized. And the Light of the great spark came now to the principle of יהוה in the mystery of the Head to all the Universes and in the mystery of HOKHMAH in the mystery of QADMON to every matter. And the upper Light is KETHER over it.

And the 2 points mentioned above, it is possible to say that they are ABBA and IMMA. But here יהוה is ABBA. And the Right Point is the mystery of IMMA in the mystery of Upper BINAH, the mystery of the house of all the reshimu from the internal colors from the Light of the Right. And the 2nd spark which we wrote above, that sparkled from the upper spark and from the points is now after the breaking the mystery of the Light that spread from the Blessed One to EYN SOF and EYN TAKHLITH to cover everything in the mystery of the Garment. And it is in the mystery of TIFERETH, in the mystery of the Spirit that covers everything. And what we wrote above in the mystery of many sparks is now in the mystery of tzimtzum – the mystery of movement. And what we wrote above from the mystery of the neshamah to all neshamoth and from the mystery of the Thought of the Primordial One of all Primordials is the Thought that thought to draw forth and engrave in it the reshimu יהוה of that was concealed. And for this reason it reduced and concealed the Light in the mystery of tip/apex of י as mentioned above. And now it is in the mystery of the Crown which MALKHUTH of ADAM QADMON. And it reduced so to speak the Light of ADAM QADMON in the mystery of the tip/apex of י as is known. In order that the 4 Universes of יהוה will be understood in actualization through the power/potential of EYN SOF between the feet of ADAM QADMON like will be explained with the help of HASHEM. And now you will understand the roots that were mentioned above. AND DO NOT THINK ANY THOUGHT OUTSIDE!!! Because all what we said until now – behold! It is only to break the ear. And all the simple/uniform Light is completely 1!

And behold, from the Light of EYN SOF until MALKHUTH of ADAM QADMON, it was not possible for the Universes to exist in actualization. And it resisted the Light of above. For example, if there is a great light, near it is a light according to its order. And it is not but the power/potential of the great light and is called by its name. Likewise, from the Light of EYN SOF until MALKHUTH of ADAM QADMON are the power/potential of the great primordial Light of above. And the matter is according to the Light that was concealed in The Blessed One in the mystery of 4 concealed colors as mentioned above. And the Light came now to the 4 levels of the primordial Light which was in the midst with the reshimu as mentioned above. And the Light of Eyn Sof is in the mystery of the Garment. And ADAM QADMON is in the mystery of YESOD. And MALKHUTH of AQ is in the mystery of the Crown. And it is the mystery of male and female within it. But the principle of the actualization of the Universes was not able to exist except from MALKHUTH of AQ and onward from the beginning to actualization. And it is known that the one who desires to build a structure needs a yesod (foundation) to erect the structure over the yesod. Likewise, so to speak, AQ is HAYESOD. The Universes were erected from the Feet[16] as is known - the bosom of the Blessed One. And from between His feet went out the shefa in the mystery of the Straight Line to the 4 Universes except in order that the Universes would be able to endure His great Light. And also for the reason that the shefa became divided into the 4 levels of the 4 Universes which became so to speak over the Universes 4 veils between the feet of the bosom of the Blessed One. And the Universes were erected over the veils over the feet of the bosom of AQ The Blessed One. And the veils are the mystery of the 4 foundations of fire, earth, water, and air. And everyone includes 4 as is known. And they are the mystery of the 3 Heads to the 4 Universes. For the 1st veil is in the mystery of the Crown of AQ. In principle, it is not counted. And in truth, there are only chief veils because the 4th veil is KETHER of Atziluth. And every veil is in the mystery of a complete stature. And they are in the mystery of garments that enclothe. And this

---

[16] 'Feet' is also a codeword for the phallus.

is the reason the Kohen needs to wear no less than 4 garments. For AQ is in the mystery of the Kohen. And the Kohen Rabba is in the mystery of the Upper Light. And the shefa that goes out from the Blessed One is enclothed in 8 garments so to speak and understand. And the reasons for the garments and their names – here is not its place[17]. And we return to the matter of the 4 veils which are in the mystery of the 4 foundations air, earth, water and fire. They were revealed in the Universe of Assiyah. From it Lower ADAM will be understood. And it has a root above in the mystery of:

"…let us make ADAM in our image…" ~ Sefer Breyshith 1:26

For 'earth/dust' is the root mystery of MALKHUTH of AQ. And it is the mystery of the root of Assiyah. And the water in adam is the sweat. And it is the mystery of AQ, the mystery of YESOD and the mystery of Yetzirah. And fire in adam is heat. It is the mystery of movement, the mystery of tzimtzum and the mystery of Briah. And the spirit/air in adam is the root of יהוה and the root of EYN SOF and the mystery of the root of Atziluth. And the veils enclothe the great Light of the 4 roots mentioned above. And when everyone

---

[17] C.F. Hayyim Vital's Eytz Hayyim Shaar 42 Chapter 1.

comes to actualization – they are able to endure it. And now we have constructed an introduction to understand the letters from the letter כ and א until ת with the help of HASHEM.

And if you find it difficult as to why the order of the letters are: אבגדהוזחטי? And accordingly, we said that the roots mentioned above were not according to this order. Because accordingly, we said that ו is hinted after י as mentioned above. And more surprisingly, the letter י is last which is unity/oneness. And it is the 1st letter of יהוה. But you need to know that the letters are according to HaSfiroth. And they hint at the oneness of The Blessed One. And behold, א, even though there exists a י over and below it and the body of א is a י (יוד) like this:

ד ו [18]י from every place. Except the tip of the י is in the mystery of KETHER. And the י at the end of

---

[18] The letter י is יוד fully spelled out, י on top, ו in the middle, and ד on

some of the letters. And both of them hint at the oneness of The Blessed One. There above is below. His essence reveals the revelation of hasadim and geburoth which hints at the letter ו as is known. Because of conjugal unions – ו mates with Upper ה, Lower ה. And they are the mystery of י. And at the time of conjugal union, י strengthens so to speak. Therefore, י is before ו and understand. And this should be enough to thee as to why ו is between ד and ז. The 10 Sfiroth are in

the mystery of a scale which are like a segolta (

) as is known – DAATH. And there exists over the segolta KETHER HOKHMAH BINAH. TIFERETH: there exists over the segolta DAATH HESED GEBURAH. MALKHUTH: There exists over the segolta so to speak NETZAH HOD YESOD. And through the conjugal unions of KETHER HOKHMAH BINAH, DAATH was born. And it is the mystery of the apex/tip of י. For example, if man speaks, then speech is born which goes out from his mouth. And if he does not speak his words except he thinks his thought, then daath is born to him in his thought via the

---

the bottom.

progression/rotation of the brains. Likewise so to speak the conjugal union of TIFERETH and MALKHUTH in the mystery of Voice and Speech. Then they give birth to actualization. And the conjugal unions of KHB are in the mystery of the brains which hint at the letter י as is known. And it gives birth to the mystery of DAATH which is the apex of י. And if so, אבג are the segolta of KHB over ד which hints to דעת (DAATH). For KETHER is in the mystery of the apex, how it is not perceived but in the mystery of DAATH which in the brains. And already we have said that from the roots of the letters and the mystery of conjugal union that what was in the mystery of DAATH is in the mystery of TIFERETH that is included and HESED and GEBURAH mate. And this is דהו as mentioned above. And afterwards, זחט hints to NETZAH HOD YESOD. Therefore ז is the number 7 since NETZAH is the 7th attribute. And ח is 8, and ט is 9. And likewise for the letters אבגדהו according to their number. And afterwards, י is alluded as mentioned above which is the 1st and it is last. And it is certainly well to understand the brevity of our words here. And from the midst of our words you will understand the entire segolta. We said they are KHB and DAATH HESED GEBURAH. And TIFERETH and MALKHUTH are not counted in the segoltas because TIFERETH is the internality as mentioned above. And it is so to speak the neshamah to HaSfiroth. Because is the segolta is only needed to break the ear so to speak. And TIFERETH is the neshamah in the mystery of DAATH. And this is the mystery of:

"…10 and not 9, 10 and not 11…" ~ *Sefer Yetzirah 1:4*

'10 and not 11' is do not divide between DAATH and TIFERETH which is do not divide God forbid between TIFERETH and MALKHUTH. And do not count God forbid MALKHUTH by herself to erect Her. And do not count 10 God forbid without it rising in thy heart except the complete unity and to make MALKHUTH in the mystery of the Crown! And TIFERETH Blessed is He unifies them all. And now we will come to explain the letter כ.

The mystery of the letter כ:

The form of the letter כ alludes to כתר (KETHER). And if you ask, why is not its property like this:

? Wouldn't this better indicate the property of KETHER? Know, that the property of KETHER according to our order is in truth like this: כ. Because the stature of the Merkabah is not like the stature of Adam from the Earth to the Heavens. Rather, the stature of the Merkabah is between the Heavens and the Earth. And this requires an exceedingly wide light. For the sphere of the Heavens and Earth are 1 sphere. And from half of the sphere and above is the Heavens. And the second half is the Earth. And all the Universes are this in the midst of that like the layers of an onion. And the entire Universe – half the sphere is the Heavens and the 2nd half is the Earth. And the line breaks the points on the horizon between Heaven and Earth. And do not wonder, if so, why the half above the line is the Heavens and the half below is the Earth. Do not wonder about this. Behold, The Name of the Blessed One Blessed is He:

"...and the night illuminates like day, like darkness so is the light." ~ Sefer Tehillim 139:12

And before the Blessed One, the Heavens and the Earth, both of them are 1 light. And He does not distinguish between them except, The Name of the Blessed One Blessed is He in His mercies, in order that they are able to endure His Light which rains on the 2nd half in the eyes of creation in order that the entire Universe is able to endure according to its arrangement. And behold, the Straight Line begins to break from AQ in the midst of the 4 Veils but in their midst the Line is not perceived until it reaches to the midst of the Universe of Atziluth. There it begins to be perceived in the mystery of the Head. And the Line extends in the mystery of ו which is ו and י above it. And the י is the face and is revealed. And its face looks to the half of the sphere of the Earth to watch over its creation. And the extension of the ו is the surrounding body. And it enclothes the 10 Sfiroth – all the Universe is enclothed. And its Light fill the entire Universe. And the extension of the ויו[19] are the internal Sfiroth in the mystery of the Scale

---

[19] One spelling of ו.

like the segolta. But in the Garment are linearity and curvature and understand. And it will be explained in another place. The straight Line breaks over this path in the midst of all 4 Universes – Atziluth is the property of ו, likewise in Briah, and likewise in Yetzirah.

And from Yetzirah the line breaks to Assiyah but not in the property of ו as mentioned above. The entire line in Assiyah is just the peduncle/tail/point from the line of Yetzirah. For the entire mass of Assiyah is with respect to Yetzirah. And it is only like the peduncle/tail/point. And the line extended from Yetzirah to Assiyah connecting Assiyah to Yetzirah. And in Assiyah the line is corporeal. And likewise it fills the entire aether/air as mentioned above. And it enclothes as mentioned above. And it extends until its end. And the line does not return to break and duly note. And afterwards, if the height goes below the horizontal line, the Merkabah is below the wings of SHEKHINAH which is below MALKHUTH. But the height of the Merkabah is the path of the horizon that separates the Heavens and the Earth from one end to the other end, from west to east. And if so, the property of KETHER is according to our path the property of כ as mentioned above and understand. And ך comes with its light, the light in itself, with the letters סודךץ with the help of HASHEM.

The mystery of the letter ל:

The letter ל is the property over the mystery of the Straight Line which is the mystery of the 3 ו's as mentioned above of Atziluth, Briah, and Yetzirah. For Assiyah is included in the peduncle of Yetzirah. And the 3 ו's are in the mystery of: Yisrael, Yaqob, and Yosef. Atziluth was constructed by the Name Yisrael which is the mystery of DAATH. Yaqob constructed Briah and Yosef Yetzirah which is the mystery of YESOD. And the peduncle connects Yetzirah with Assiyah which connects YESOD with MALKHUTH. And a wondrous hint to this is in our Holy Torah. 'Breyshith' begins with a ב, the 2nd book with ו, the 3rd book Waykra with ו, the 4th book with ו, and the 5th book Debarim with א – behold! בוווא which in gematria = אהיה (21) which hints at the ב which is half of the right sphere of the breaking of the circle which was divided as mentioned in length. And it is the mystery of the Universe resembling an exedra and from the side of the North an opening. And the 3 ו's hint at the Line that breaks in the midst of the ב in the mystery of Yisrael Yaqob Yosef. And the א alludes to EYN SOF. And it alludes to the fact that He is the 1st and the Last. And we return to the matter. The property of ל is the property of the Straight Line. ויו (a spelling of ו) over ל certainly hints to the Line of Atziluth.

And it is not perceived as much as in Briah. The 2nd ו is wider in extension which hints at the Line in Briah. There the light is perceived. And the 3rd ו comes like a pen. Accordingly, this Line hints to Yetzirah and Assiyah because the apex/tip/end breaks from the Universe of Yetzirah to Assiyah. And accordingly, it hints to the 2 Universes which are not extended equally except circular like a pen.

The mystery of the letter מ:

The letter מ is open. It is the form י ו כ. And it is open below. And the matter of each and every Universe is in the mystery of כ. And each and every Universe the Line breaks as mentioned above. And the line in each Universe is in the mystery of י and ו as mentioned above. And in truth, after Briah, the Line is enclothed in the midst of the Universe in order that the Lower Ones are able to endure this Universe. But we speak in the mystery of the letters which hint at the order of Briah. And accordingly, the order of the Line is before the Universe. And it enlivens the Universe. And over this, is the property of the letter open מ. And it is open below in order that the Line extends from Universe to Universe below it.

The mystery of the letter ב:

The letter נ is in the mystery of the breaking[20] of the circle and the breaking is like this:

But it was symmetrical, so it was not possible to erect the Universes because Right and Left were equal. And in order for the Right to overpower the Left, the essence of the strengthening needs to be below the foundation of the Universes. Therefore, below the Right נ, all the foundation is until the extension of the Line of the left side[21]. And we find that it was made from the mystery of breaking bent נ and straight ן. And in the future, when the

---

[20] Many of the principal Lurianic texts vary as to the letters used for the breaking. Letters referenced are ב, נ, and ח. This text is unique, in that it is aware of all these esoteric levels, and seems to unify them all by explaining them as different facets of the breaking.

[21] The passage is very obscure here. Moreover, it is possible the image we have may not be a true representation of what the author had in mind given the limitation of ancient printing presses. In my humble understanding, I think the key to understanding has to do with the bases of the right and left נ's. The key being that the base of the right נ is longer than the left נ.

Accuser is sweetened, everything will be in the mystery of Right. And straight ו will be enclothed in bent נ. And it will be in the mystery of closed ם. And the Universe will be completely complete. May it be hastily in our days amen.

The mystery of the letter ס:

The letter ס is in the mystery of tzimtzum of EYN SOF Blessed is HE with His essence so to speak. It was in the mystery of EYN SOF and EYN TAKHLITH bringing into existence a place for the Universes in His midst. And this place has an end. And therefore, the tzimtzum hints at the letter ס. Accordingly, it is the form of the tzimtzum. And also, ס is the 1st letter of the word סוף (end). And the letter ס is in the mystery of the womb so to speak to bring forth in its midst the Universes without end and number.

The mystery of the letters פ,צ,ע:

The letter ע – behold! Make thy ear like the grain receiver because it is impossible to lengthen about this. The mystery of Alohim is a concealed matter. And it requires understanding a matter in the midst of a matter. Know, that:

"...from the phallus/flesh I see ALWAH (The Goddess)." ~ Sefer Iyob 19:26

And behold, when the tzimtzum was in the mystery of EYN SOF as mentioned above, it was in the mystery of the womb. And already we said above at the beginning, we spoke a parable that the body is apportioned to 4 levels. And the 3rd portion is the portion of the womb. And the 4th portion is the portion of the covenant (phallus) and thighs. And when the 3rd [level] from the portion of the body was erected, the power of man was completed. He needed to engage in conjugal union. Arousal came through the power of the Primordial One who spread below. And He is the mystery of י, the mystery of the male. And the light of EYN SOF tzimtzum (contracted) itself so to speak. Above was the mystery of movement. And it moves itself and distanced itself so to speak with the Light of the upper power. And it is the mystery of male and female cleaving together in the mystery of 'lovers who never separate'. And the movements were in the mystery of Lower י. And even though the movements rose above and the upper power spread itself below so to speak. In any case, the movements were not just with respect to pleasure[22]. And the Power is Upper י. And the movements are of the Lower י of the letter א. And behold, in the middle is the body of the male like we wrote at the beginning of our words. And

---

[22] The highest archetypal divine orgasm to speak.

behold, now you will understand the letter ע over its properties because until now we have spoken from the letter א until ס. And most of the stature was not yet complete so to speak of the power of the male. And there was no sexual arousal to actualize the Universes. And everything was in the mystery of אלף (א spelled out) – the letters פלא (concealed) and He was concealed. But now after the tzimtzum, ע was made from א. Because Lower י is in the mystery of movement going above to pleasure (orgasm). For the form of ע is like the form of א except Lower י is in the letter א at the time of pleasure (orgasm). And sexual union is strengthened with respect to Upper י. And it became the form of ע. And the body of ע is like the form of ו like in the letter א except it is bent. And a curtain covers before the sexual union so to speak. And the letter ע is an aid. And when you add the right י of the letter ע with the extension of the body of ע it is the form of a bent נ.. And the letter י in its midst is male and female. And the right י of the letter ע is taller in comparison to the 2nd י. Accordingly at the time of sexual orgasm, it strengthens over it. And even though י is the mystery of the male, it is above, and the נ supports the י. And the know that the letters ע פ צ are פצע (a wound). It wishes to say that when male and female are sexually aroused and cleaving, and the male is strengthened, from this power so to speak, the פצע of male and female is made. And He is in the mystery of the Mouth because the reshimu of the letter פ is a chain of sexual embrace. And from the power of strengthening, in it was made a splitting in the mystery of the mouth. And behold, the letter ב is also likewise in the mystery of the female as stated above. Except ב is in the mystery of BINAH and in the mystery of the Brains. And the Power was not born until the most of the stature was complete. And now the י from the Brains spread below in order that sexual union would not be revealed. And the י was in the midst of the Mouth. And the power was brought forth in the mystery of the Phallus YESOD of the Female. And it connected with the mystery of the of the Male. And when it is the mystery of the Mouth it is the mystery of the Tabernacle in the mystery of the Tabernacle and afterwards the vessels. And it was spreading from above so to speak from the Brains in the mystery of the 2 י's Male and Female in the mystery of the 2 testicles. And it became the mystery of YESOD. And it is the form of the letter צ YESOD OLAM. It is the חי (18th) letter from the letter א until צ in the mystery of Eternal חי (LIFE). Because the form of the letter is like this:

And this form is the form of ע, except the line is extended a bit wide in the hoof. And the matter is because the property of ע alludes to sexual arousal in the Brains. And the letter צ is YESOD of the Brains. And there is no difference in צ except the extension of the hoof in order that it will be concealed. And if it is difficult to thee why the Mouth is before the letter צ, already we mentioned that it is the mystery of the Tabernacle and afterwards the vessels. And if in the beginning, צ was in the mystery of YESOD, there would be GEBUROTH and God forbid the waters of hasadim would be annulled. Therefore the Tabernacle was made in the beginning and understand. And through this you will understand the letters צפע. And now we will explain the letters קרשת.

The mystery of the letter ק:

The letter ק is 2 Thighs from the Primordial One to every matter. The Universes stood over them. And already we said above, through the mystery of engraving, the Light was purified and the Supreme Power from the colors until the external colors which remained in the mystery of the Backs. They are in the mystery of a linen sheet. And they did not have the power to find grasping in order to arouse and mix with the internal Light. And now afterwards, it became the mystery of Life, the mystery of holy sexual union so to speak. It remained over the linen sheet in the mystery of the last drop and they found grasping and were aroused. And for this reason they found grasping between the 2 Thighs – the place of sexual union. For this reason, She has grasping until the Universe of Briah. It wishes to say until MALKHUTH of Atziluth as is known. For the ground of Atziluth is the mystery of the last drop. And they were in the mystery of a linen sheet. Therefore, they had grasping until the ground of Atziluth. Because the 3 Universes Briah, Yetzirah, and Assiyah stand over the 2 Thighs. And the Thighs are the foundations of the Universes Briah, Yetzirah, and Assiyah. And in the Thighs they have grasping. Therefore, they have grasping in the Universes Briah, Yetzirah, and Assiyah. But the Universe of Atziluth is in the mystery of the Womb. And there they do not have grasping. And with this you will understand the form of the letter ק. The extension of the encircling line hints over the ground of Atziluth. And the extension of the foot hints at the Externalities. Accordingly, the essence of their grasping is in the left Thigh. Therefore there exists to the letter ק one foot and it is to the left side. And already it has been made known to thee that the Straight Line hints at the 3 ו's of Sefer Shmoth 14:19-21[23]. And in the Universe of Assiyah there does not exist ו but the peduncle/apex of Yetzirah it fills. They have grasping in 2 ו's. And it is not intended in the body of ו God forbid except on the left side of the orgasm of the ו in its Externalities.

The mystery of the letter ד:

The 2 ו's are in the mystery of ד as mentioned above[24] with the letter ג. This alludes to the letter ד.

The mystery of the letter ש:

Behold, ש alludes to the form of the property of the 3 ו's. From the Power, the internal Lines have sexual intercourse. From this Power comes to them the grasping in the mystery of the last drop. And it is the engraving of the holy drops that hint at the

---

[23] That make up the 72 Divine Letter Name.
[24] Don't recall this being mentioned above. Either way this section on this letter makes no sense to me!

letter ש. Therefore, the reason the Externalities think they have power over the 3 ו's. But it is deception. Therefore the 3 letters deceive. They stand this after that because they [the Externalities] do not have except waste.

The mystery of the letter ת:

And with all this, it comes afterwards the letter ת. And it is the seal of HQBH. For His seal is אמת (TRUTH). First, middle, and end[25]. And hints likewise at the word מות mentioned above. The Qlippoth will be burned from the Universe because it will be in the mystery of sealed ם as mentioned above.

Finished and completed. Praise to El the Creator of the Universe.

---

[25] The Hebrew word for 'truth' is made up of the first, middle, and last letters of the Alef-Beth.

TOSEFTA:

Extracts From: The Principal Shabbathian Commentary to Sifra Detziunatha

Folio 6B Lines 2 – 27:

"The second Earth was not in the calculation...and from this it was cursed..." ~ *Sifra Detziunatha [Sefer HaZohar 2:176B]*

And in order to explain this matter, we will explain the beginning of the matter a little of the Thoughtful Light and the Thoughtless light and why it is called by this name. Essentially, it is known that before the spreading when it was in the mystery of qutra begolma (the binding of formlessness[i]) it was yet Thoughtless Light included in potential and not actualized in Lower SHEKHINAH so to speak…Indeed, when it rose in the will of Alohey Yisrael which is Upper Thought to spread, He spread from ATIQA of all Atiqin The Concealed of all Concealments. And behold, ATIQA is in the mystery of KETHER the Head of Thought above in the mystery of [ii]א as explained above with the matter of the 7 Tiqqunim of the Head[iii]. And everything is in the mystery of Upper Thought. And it spread until the mystery of TIFERETH. Above was Alohey Yisrael Blessed is He in the mystery of Thought by Himself and in His Glory. And from there until TIFERETH it spread except its Holy Light. And when it arose in His Will to spread above towards ATIQA of Atiqin The Concealed of all Concealments to receive, then His Light was gathered from the midst of TIFERETH to His place mentioned above – the Upper Thought which is in the mystery of א as mentioned above. And there His Light rose from the midst of TIFERETH in the mystery of the encircling Light to Upper Thought. And Thought is the middle Light dwelling in TIFERETH.

Therefore, this Light is called the Thoughtful Light. Because in it dwells Thought until the Light rises above to encircle Thought as mentioned above. There it receives from the Root. And ATIQA of Atiqin so to speak is in the mystery of sexual union. Indeed, before the tiqqun when it was not yet in sexual union as mentioned above in the mystery of the Divine Scale as mentioned above, Alohey Yisrael was so to speak building the Universes and there was no existence[iv] as mentioned above as mentioned above. And then He brought out the Thoughtless Light in the mystery of a holy shadow strengthening the judgments from potential to actualization as mentioned above in the mystery of 'the Qlippah come before the fruit'. Indeed, when they strengthened afterwards the judgments increased the shefa without balance causing the breaking of the vessels as mentioned above. And afterwards when it was rectified, and 7 Tiqqunnim of the Head were rectified/established with the 13 Tiqqunnim of the Divine Beard. In order to be that from then and onward the entire structure of the Universes would be via sexual union. And Alohey Yisrael Blessed is He rose His Light dwelling in TIFERETH above to encircle Thought as mentioned above in the mystery of א as mentioned above in the mystery of:

"…a woman shall encompass a man." ~ Sefer Yirmeyahu 31:22

To receive above in the mystery of the Divine Scale/Balance. Then this precious Light raises the Thoughtful Light because in it dwells the Upper Thought. And indeed, the Light which Alohey Yisrael brought out is in the mystery of a shadow encircling holiness and in the mystery of the Qlippah as mentioned above. And it was not able to rise with Alohey Yisrael to encircle Thought as mentioned above except it remained below as mentioned above….therefore the Light is called the Thoughtless Light because it does not rise to encircle Thought and it does not contain the Thought of above. And when it saw that it was impossible for it to rise like the Thoughtful Light it became jealous in the mystery of the Serpent which was jealous of Adam. And it caused the first Adam to sin. And He cast it into the depths of the Sea as mentioned in Sefer HaZohar Parashath Breyshith[v]. Therefore, afterwards, at the time of rectification, it was not included with the rest of the Tiqun of of the Beard until the time of the true restoration, may it be hastened in our days! For this, it was said 'and the second Earth' which is the Thoughtful Light which is in the mystery of the 2nd Earth like a shadow to

Lower SHEKHINAH who is the 2ⁿᵈ Earth in the mystery of the depths of the Sea. And it was not in the calculation/counting of the Tiqunnim. Because from this it was cursed which is to say that from it went out curses to the Universe as mentioned above. And therefore it was not rectified. Therefore, the Thoughtless Light is continually accusing in the mystery of jealousy as mentioned above which desires to rise like the Thoughtful Light. And indeed it is not able to rise except until ATIQA who is in the mystery of Thought because it does not spread via Thought except via its Light that dwells in TIFERETH.

"Give wisdom to a wise man…" ~ Proverbs 9:9

By itself and by itself it will be explained.

Folios 10A-B:

It is known that at the time of Creation of the Universe before the spreading and revelation of the י of Alohey Yisrael so to speak, He included ATTIQA in the mystery of folding[vi] inside the amniotic sac which encircled the 2 Shekhinoth in the midst of 2 ד's which encircle like the closed ם like this:

[vii]

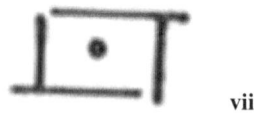

Here comes the form of the 2 letters ד which one is reversed. And these forms form a square. And in the middle is a point in the mystery of:

"Blessed is the man who heareth me watching daily at [viii] דלתתי (my gates) day day…" ~ *Proverbs 8:34*

And they encircle Alohey Yisrael so to speak in the mystery of the amniotic sac that encircles a child from all sides because it is then in the mystery of a infant in the bowels of his mother as is known in the mystery of infancy and the mystery of folding 3 in 3[ix] in enclothement[x]. And the initiated will understand. And likewise in the mystery of internality. And then it did not bestow the shefa to them in the mystery of TIFERETH except in the mystery of YESOD in the mystery of TZADDIQ YESOD עולם (OLAM)[xi] – עול ם (infant of ם) as in:

"Can a woman forget her עולה (suckling child)?..." ~ *Sefer Yeshayahu 49:15*

ב is YESOD of the amniotic sac as recalled above. And as is known that YESOD is called the Child of delights. And in the mystery that:

"When he was a child of Yisrael (NAAR YISRAEL[xii]) and I made sexual love to him." ~ Sefer Hoshea 11:1[xiii]

And then his mother was included. Likewise, the inner י's which are in the midst of the 2 ה's of the 2 SHEKHINOTH – the mystery of the primordial Light. The spirit that is bequeathed upon Her husband[xiv]. The mystery of the 2 י's of the Divine Scale mentioned above. They were concealed furthermore at the time of infancy and the initiated will understand[xv]. And yet they are His mother in the mystery of:

"Light is sown for TZADDIQ…" ~ Sefer Tehillim 97:11

The primordial Light mentioned above. In order that the Thoughtless Light does not suckle from them which is to say the evil powers that encircle the amniotic sac and desire to suckle from this. Like the Arizal states:

"And Alohim saw the light that it was good…" ~ Sefer Breyshith 1:4

And He concealed the אור (Light) – רז (the mystery) – YESOD[xvi]. As mentioned above,

Alohey Yisrael was then in the mystery of YESOD and YESOD is the mystery of י as is known in the Zohar[xvii]. י is Alohey Yisrael and ATTIQA QADISHA included in the mystery of י as recalled above. And His mother concealed the 2 י's of the Primordial Light. Behold, 3 י's are included in י. 1 is in the mystery of the 3 tips of י and the mystery of the 3 drops of Segolta (the Niqqud). And everything was included in 1 י in the midst of the amniotic sac which is the mystery of the Mother. And in the mystery of:

"…1 She is to the Mother…" ~ Shir HaShirim 6:9

Folios 8A-9A:

And behold, from the beginning there were 2 Serpents. 1 is the mystery of the Holy Serpent as mentioned above. And 1 is in the mystery of the external Serpent – the Thoughtless Light which is in the mystery of the image of Holiness. And it encircles in the mystery of the '2nd Earth'. And afterwards:

"…reverting to 1…" ~ Sifra Detziunatha [Sefer HaZohar 2:176B]

Via the waters of the Great Sea. At the time of the breaking, it reached to it the flood of many waters [Sefer Tehillim 32:6]. And then the head of the External Serpent was broken in the mystery of Sefer Breyshith 3:15. And it bruised its head! And then the Good from them was drawn to King Mashiah in the mystery of the 'and the spirit of Alohim hovered[xviii]' – this is the spirit of King Mashiah[xix] which is the internality as is known. And the rest was rejected below. And HQBH took it to the depths of the sea as is recalled in Sefer HaZohar Parashath Breyshith 19B as mentioned above. See there. And King Mashiah, his external garment is the mystery of the tail as mentioned above to force and reject them below as mentioned above. And therefore, this garment is likewise in the mystery of the '2nd Earth'. He was sent there to bring out the sparks as is known in the mystery of:

"...and the serpent – dust/earth shall be its food..." ~ Sefer Yeshayahu 65:25

The mystery of the '2nd Earth'. And He was able to enter there because:

"...from this it was cursed..." ~ Sifra Detziunatha [Sefer HaZohar 2:176B]

And behold, the inner light of the Serpent is the mystery of the Staff/Wand in the mystery of:

"…and the spirit of Alohim…" ~ Sefer Breyshith 1:2

Which is the mystery of ו which is the internal spirit. And the Externalities are in the mystery of the Serpent as recalled above. Therefore, the exile of Mitzrayim was in order that they would believe how He would be able to redeem them in 210 years before the prescribed time[xx]. And how the Holy Light went out from the Thoughtless Light. He showed them Mushah who is in the mystery of King Mashiah with the wand in his hand which transformed into the Serpent which is the Holy Serpent as mentioned above. And he went there and Mushah brought out everything as mentioned above via the hole of the head of the Dragon that is mentioned in Sefer HaZohar[xxi] Parashat Wara 2:27B, 28A, and 30B on the explanations of the Dragons. And this is its language:

"'You broke the heads of the dragons over the waters…' ~ Sefer Tehillim 74:13

All of their spirits breathe upwards." ~ Zohar 2:34B

See there. (As recalled above in the mystery of the 'spirit of Alohim hovers'[xxii]). Indeed, פרעה (Pharoah) who was near Him was the exile of SHEKHINAH as is known in the mystery of ה

עפר (the Dust of ה)ˣˣⁱⁱⁱ. It relies upon the majority of the power of the External Serpent – the mystery of the Thoughtless Light. The Dragon lies in the midst of His riversˣˣⁱᵛ. And therefore, He commanded to send there Mushah in the mystery of fallen ה, fallen ו, after He raises Her as is recalled many times in Sefer HaZoharˣˣᵛ. Which was then in the mystery of King Mashiah the fallen Sonˣˣᵛⁱ in the mystery of the garment and internality. And He arose above in the mystery of 'and the Spirit of Alohim hovered'. Therefore, His ark was seen 'over the face of the waters'. And the initiated will understand. And therefore, likewise the magicians of Mitrayim did with their magikh in transformingˣˣᵛⁱⁱ...in the mystery of the External Serpent.

"...Alohim hath set this opposing that..." ~ Sefer Qoheleth 7:14

And when Mushah saw this, he was exceedingly afraid that the External Serpent did not cleave to him God forbid via the increase of the lights that fell in his midst. The Holy Serpent is the mystery of his wand like it was at the hour of the Creation of the Universeˣˣᵛⁱⁱⁱ. And in particular because then he had uncircumcised lips [according to Shmoth 6:12]. Because they grasped [the evil powers] his garment when they were sent to the Nile/river and took from Him his words. SHEKHINAH is the mystery of 'His word' as is recalled in Sefer HaZohar Parashat Wara; see there[xxix]. And there is recalled the saying of the Dragons. Mushah was exceedingly afraid because of the Great Dragon. And He did not desire to war against Him[xxx] as mentioned above. And HQBH said to Him 'do not fear except take it by the tail' [according to Shmoth 4:4] which is the tail of the Holy Serpent as recalled above. Hard judgment is His external garment. And he went there and crushed their heads in the mystery Breyshith 3:15 'and He bruised the head', in order for the spirits to breath to draw[xxxi] the inner Good Light in them in the mystery of 'and the Spirit of Alohim'…In the mystery of the wand of Mushah as recalled above towards the internality of the Holy Serpent which is likewise in the mystery of the Wand. And then it said [Shmoth 4:4] 'the staff was in his palm' which is the internality of the Holy Serpent – the mystery of the Wand. His palm is the mystery of [his] formation by the palm of HQBH[xxxii]. Because the Serpent is the external garment that goes to crush the head of the Serpent-Dragon to bring out its light. And then:

"...and the wand of Aharon swallowed their wands." ~ Shmoth 7:12

Which is the inner light that goes out from them as mentioned above. And everything was done via the wand of Aharon! And not via the wand of Mushah. It was recalled above that Mushah was exceedingly afraid lest the Externalities grasp him since he was yet in the mystery of uncircumcised lips as mentioned above. And the initiated will understand. And the mystery of this hole in the head:

"All of their spirits breathe upwards." ~ Zohar 2:34B

Is the mystery of MALKHUTH the House of Dawid. They had a hole in their head in the mystery of 'The one who has the KETHER of MALKHUTH of Beth Dawid is suitable when known that he is from the seed of Dawid' as is found in Talmud Babli[xxxiii]. And in the Zohar[xxxiv] in the mystery of King Mashiah who has a hole in the head as mentioned above. And this is the mystery of Rab Yiba Saba who is the mystery of King Mashiah as is known. The word Saba, its root is in ATTIQA who is called Saba de Sabin (The Elder of Elders). When He resembled an Arab donkey driver, he asked them:

"Who is the Serpent that flies in the Aether?"xxxv (Which is Holy Serpent mentioned above that flies in the aether above and is not known) and goes in separation. He goes in a separated place in the mystery of the 'Fallen Son'. "And between hither and between thither rests one ant lying between his teeth". [Until here]. And it is known in many places that King Mashiah encircles Lower SHEKHINAH which is the mystery of the antxxxvi which hoardeth her food in the summer. As is known in the mystery of xxxvii ש. King Mashiah is the mystery of the ב [here was added an image] – The Holy Serpent encircles internal ש of ו [the letter is written large]. The ו is the internality of Lower ה between her ascent above to have sexual relations, between her existence below in the mystery of exile 'the fallen one'. For this reason it was said: "between hither and between thither there rests…". 'Between' – her ascent above to have sexual relations. 'Between thither' – her existence below in the mystery of exile for our many iniquities. 'And there rests one ant' – Lower SHEKHINAH. 'Lying between his teeth' – the mystery of ש and She is ו lying between 2 teeth of ב like this: שׁ. 'She rests' [which is to say shelter] from the suckling of the

Thoughtless Light. And also the Holy Serpent is the Serpent that bites the pudendum of the Doe at the time of giving birth as is known. And therefore She is called the Ant that lies between the teeth. This is the Holy Serpent. And See it was said by Rab Yiba Saba:

"What is that that begins in union and ends in separation?" ~ Sefer HaZohar 2:95A

'Begins in union' – The beginning of the ו [maybe a mistake, instead it should be] surrounds Upper Holiness which is called 'union'. And there He connects the aspect of the good inner Light. 'Ends in separation' – the end and His garment in the mystery of the end and tail which is separated. Which is to say He supports the Thoughtless Light[xxxviii]. Or you may explain 'begins in union' as in the beginning at the time of Creation, there were 2 Serpents in union as mentioned above. 'And ends in separation' – Because:

"...reverting to 1..." ~ Sifra Detziunatha [Sefer HaZohar 2:176B]

And He draws to Him all the Light of the Good. In the mystery of:

"The wicked is prepared but the tzaddiq is enclothed..." ~ Sefer Iyob 27:17[xxxix]

And the Thoughtless Light was rejected below in the mystery of:

"The second Earth was not in the calculation…and from this it was cursed…" ~ *Sifra Detziunatha [Sefer HaZohar 2:176B]*

Below is a highly esoteric unpublished verse from the Apocrypha of HaMashiah Yaqob Frank!!!

"For they knew also regarding the Holy Serpent that protects the Garden. Is the path to it not even known by the Bird!?[xl] And ye asked what is the Serpent doing in the Garden of Eden? He is the Serpent that is found continually in the Garden of Eden. And whoever touches Him merits eternal lives!"

Annotations to TOSEFTA:

---

[i] C.F. Sefer Zohar 1:15A
[ii] At the beginning of the commentary, it is stated that א denotes the Divine Scale.
[iii] The Ancient of Days.
[iv] According to Breyshith Rabbah 3:7
[v] C.F. 1:19B
[vi] C.F. Sefer Emeq HaMelekh Gates 1-3.
[vii] To my knowledge, this is the only book that contains such an image. Very interestingly, Rab Mushah David Valle in his Sefer Liqutim also has a section with this image and an explanation very similar to what is found here proving indeed that He was a Shabbathian/Frankist Grandmaster!
[viii] The full spelling of the word ד.
[ix] C.F. Sefer Emeq HaMelekh and Hayyim Vital's works en passim.
[x] See the parable in Hayyim Vital's Shaar Kawanoth – the matter of Pesah – Explanation א.
[xi] Proverbs 10:25
[xii] A Partzuf of Zeir Anpin.
[xiii] Actual esoteric translation!
[xiv] This spirit is bequeathed upon husband and wife at the time of their first sexual relations according to Sefer HaZohar. C.F. Sefer HaZohar 2:99B. The ARI also speaks like this about the spirit of the divine partzufim. C.F. Hayyim Vital's Gate 39 Explanation א.
[xv] They are the internality of the 2 SHEKHINOTH. And 1 of them is identical to the neshamah of Mashiah.
[xvi] C.F. Sefer HaZohar 2:169B And the gematria of 'light' and 'mystery' are equal. To this, C.F. Sefer HaZohar Raaya Mehemna 3:15B.
[xvii] C.F. Zohar 1:56A
[xviii] Sefer Breyshith 1:2
[xix] C.F. ancient Midrashim to verse.
[xx] See Rashi to Breyshith 15:13
[xxi] Also C.F. Zohar 2:34B
[xxii] This verse is explained in the Zohar at the end of the folio. And this explanation is explained in Nathan of Gaza's 'Treatise on Dragons'. It is intended to 'Shabbathai Tzbi' which in gematria is equal to 'Alohim hovers'!
[xxiii] C.F. Sefer Yeshayahu 52:2 which is a veiled reference to our Holy Goddess! This formulation of permutation is also used in our infamous

Qabbalistic hymn 'Lekha Dodi'.

[xxiv] C.F. Sefer Yekhezel 29:3

[xxv] Not found. Similar ideas are seen in Sefer HaZohar 2:241B, 3:75A, 3:293B (Idra Zuta), 2:116A (Raaya Mehemna). Also in Sefer Tiqquney Zohar Tiqqun 19 42A and Tiqqun 21 53A.

[xxvi] C.F. Talmud Babli Tractate Sanhedrin 96B

[xxvii] C.F. Sefer Shmoth 7:11

[xxviii] At the beginning of the emanation of the Universe, good and evil were mixed together.

[xxix] C.F. 2:25B

[xxx] C.F. Zohar 2:34A

[xxxi] The root of this word is sometimes used in HaZohar to the idea of the spirit leaving the body. See 3:270B (Matnitin). But this principle is found certainly of 'entering' of the spirit to the body. See the parable in 3:141A (Idra Rabba).

[xxxii] C.F. See the parable in Pesiktha Rabbathi: 'lest you are greater than man whom I formed with mine own palms.'

[xxxiii] Not found. But C.F. Sefer HaZohar 1:110B Sitrei Torah regarding 'the crown of Milkam' upon King Dawid.

[xxxiv] C.F. Zohar 1:173A 'Engraved upon the crown of Milkam was the Serpent.' C.F. 2:107A 'The image of the God of the Ammonites was a crooked Serpent engraved upon their Swords.' C.F. 1 Shamuel 11:1. Milkam is from the Hebrew root 'melekh' which also signifies 'counsel' as in the 'counsel of the serpent' found in Talmud Babli Tractate Shabbath 55B.

[xxxv] C.F. Sefer HaZohar 2:95A

[xxxvi] Permutation of 2 verses: Proverbs 6:8 and 10:5.

[xxxvii] This letter signifies teeth.

[xxxviii] In the Zohar the Universe of Separation as opposed to the Universe of Unification. See the parable in Sefer HaZohar 2:234A.

[xxxix] The verse is cited as such in the Gemara to Talmud Babli Tractates Baba Metzia 61B and Baba Qamma 119A. And so in the Zohar 2:108B.

[xl] Allusion to Sefer Iyob 28:20-21

כוללת הקדמה

וראש תוך, סוף היינו, תלת בסוד היא נקודה כל כי נודע הנה העניין להבין. אמצעים ומים תחתונים מים, עליונים מים בסוד העניין כי דע (כו,ט איוב) "אלוה אחזה מבשרי" כי משל צריך לו נופל מתחילה, משל דרך. ורצון חכמה, מחשבה דרך על הוא אם מחשבה באותה מתחכם כ"ואה במחשבתו דבר לאדם אל אותה יוציא אם ולאו גם ואם הפועל אל אותה להוציא עד מחשבה ובאותה. וכמה ואיך תהיה עניין באיזה הפועל אזי הנכונה הדרך שחישב ואחר אצלו נכון שיותר מה שמחשב כאן נמצאו. הפועל אל דבר אותו להוציא חזק מוסכם לו יש הם ושלושתם ורצון חכמה, מחשבה: במחשבה מדרגות שלוש והיא "ראשונה מחשבה" נקראת הראשונה מחשבה כי במוח ומדרגה ה,] "מקל להלון" "הקדומים לכל קדומה מחשבה" סתם "קדומה מחשבה" הנקראת המחשבה חכמה היא השניה אל בא מן המחשבה ו"המחשבה רצון" היא השלישית ומדרגה מחשבה: מדרגות תלת שיש וכמו. הפועל אל הכח ומן הכח מחשבה: מדרגות תלת ישנן כן כמו, למחשבה ורצון חכמה, במחשבה שיהיה שמה באופן בפועל וכן בכח ורצון חכמה ניכרת ואז הפועל אל הכח ומן הכח אל בא גדול בהעלם ורצונו ומחשבתו הפועל כח ניכר הפעולה ומתוך. לכל הפעולה משל שעל תראה המשל בזה תשכיל ואם. המשל כאן עד הטוב סוד הם ב"כח. מ"נהי ת"חג ב"כח ספירות עשר עניין יובנו זה סוד גם ושלושתם המחשבה ורצון קדומה ומחשבה ה"מקל הוא י"ונה בכח ורצון חכמה, מחשבה סוד הוא ת"חג. המחשבה הפעולה גמר היא ומלכות בפועל [ורצון חכמה, מחשבה] סוד כי ודע. תחילה במחשבה מעשה סוף, הכתר בסוד העטרה בסוד דאתכסיא עלמא ב"כח סוד הוא ה"י, ה, ה"ב ה'הוי הקדוש השם וברתא ברא סוד והוא דאתגליא עלמא סוד הוא ה"ו ואותיות

79

שהוא הפועל בערך היינו, הכח הוא ת"שחג שאמרנו פ"ואע
הפועל ערך ת"חג נקראים דאתכסיא עלמא בערך אבל מ"נהי.
אות מחשבת של ורצון חכמה מחשבה הם ב"כח נאמר כן ואם
של ורצון חכמה מחשבה וערך ברא הנקרא תפארת שהוא ו'
בערך הרצון היא שבינה פ"אע ת"חג בינה היא ו' אות פעולת
המחשבה חכמת חסד. ה"המקל היא הפעולה לערך המחשבה
היא ותפארת הפעולה לערך והכל המחשבה רצון גבורה
לפעולת ורצון חכמה מחשבה שהם גבורה חסד בינה. הפעולה
של ורצון חכמה המחשבה בערך ברתא סוד ה' לאות הם ו' אות
בחסד ה' אות מחשבת של ה"המקל בבינה היינו ה' אות המחשבה
ה' אות רצון בגבורה ה' אות של סתם קדומה מחשבה
מחשבה הם יסוד נצח תפארת. ה' אות מחשבת של ושלושתם
והוד ונצח הפעולה היא ה' ואות ה' אות פעולת של ורצון חכמה
בסוד הם הדינים אחיזת עיקר כי נודע כי לאחת נחשבים הם
שכל נודע וכבר. חיצוניות דעת סוד והוא שלו בחיצוניות
שכתבנו מה וכל תכלית ואין סוף אין עד מעשר כלולה ספירה
ופעולת ו' אות מחשבת של ורצון 3 חכמה למחשבה כלל דרך
וכמו בכתר לך תצטייר. ה' אות ופעולת ה' אות ומחשבת ו' אות
בינה למה תקשה ואל. הספירות בכל כ"וכ ובבינה בחכמה כן
ובאות ו' אות לפעולת ה"ומקל ו' אות למחשבת הרצון סוד היא
לפי, לפעולה ה"המקל ותפארת למחשבה הרצון היא הגבורה ה'
ומשם החכמה עם מתפרשין דלא רעין תרין בסוד היא שבינה
הרצון היא המחשבה בערך לפיכך. ק"לו ומשפעת מקבלת
בעצמותו שנעלם ה' אות אבל. ה"המקל היא הפעולה ובערך
אין כביכול הקצוות מן ולפועל למחשבה יוצא כשהוא יתברך
שהבינה מה כי אחת פעם רק [אלא] פעמים שתי גבורה לחשוב
תתאה שכינתא לייחד הכוונה עיקר ה"מקל לפעולת נחשוב
[מלכות] מעשה סוף להיות [בינה] עילאה בשכינתא [מלכות]
שאחיזת שאמרנו מה כי דע גם. והבן [בינה] תחילה במחשבה
באמת כי העולמות בכל ו"ח הכוונה אין, בהוד הם הדינים

היין סוד הוא וגבורה המשומר יין סוד דינים מתערי מבינה יצר הוא חמץ סוד והוא. היין חומץ סוד הוא והוד באתגלייא ותבין ו"ח העולמות בכל זה אין אבל חיצוניות מחשבת הרע עולמות 'בד הקדוש השם הוא המרכבה כל באמת כי בזה עולם כלל דרך כן ואם ה"ב ה'הוי סוד הם עולמות 'וד ע"אבי דרך מ"מ ס"א עד לעשר שבפרטו פ"אע, האצילות בקוץ המחשבה סוד 'י סוד הוא האצילות עולם כל הכללי. ה' הרצון סוד הוא בכללו הבריאה ועולם היוד בגוף והחכמה הבינה פירוש וגבורה גדולה בסוד הקצוות הם ובינה, עליונה 'ו סוד הוא בכללו היצירה עולם וכל. וגבורות חסדים כוללת תפארת שוכן ובו גבורות 'וה חסדים 'ה הכולל תפארת הוד הוא האצילות כל כלל דרך כן כי דחכמה תפארת והוא דאצילות סוד הוא בכללו העשיה עולם וכל כנזכר חכמה שהיא היוד סוד ספירות עשר מחלקים כשאנחנו כן ואם. אחרונה 'ה סוד מלכות מיצירה מ"ב נהי ספירות מתחילין אזי העולמות כללות דרך רק אחיזה להם אין דיצירה בבריאה אפילו כן ואם דיצירה 'ו שהוא בתפארת השוכן אור ו"ח מסתלק עבירה י"ע לפעמים הסתר ואנכי" כדכתיב פנים הסתרת בסוד כביכול דיצירה ואז החכמה אור שהוא העינים בסילוק( )יח,לא דברים "אסתיר עד ולפעמים בבריאה שלהם השורש עד הדינים מתגברים ו"ח ויש השגה שום להם אין ולמעלה משם אבל דאצילות קרקרע עניין מהן]לקמן[דאתוון ברזא מבואר והוא גדול סוד בזה לא ובזה מהם שנברר גוונין הארבע כח על שהוא הקטרוג באצילות לא אבל הכח סוד שהוא הבריאה עת עד כבר הרגישו עושים וכשאנו ראש לה אין 'שהקלי לפי מחשבה סוד שהוא כביכול המחשבה אור מורידים אנו אזי מקום של רצונו עד דחי אל מדחי אותם ומדחים הדינים וממתקים ומבררים במדרגה רק הדינים נשארו ולא בכללו העולם שיוטהר תחתיות סוד שהוא התחתונה

והשתלשלות גליפין דאתוון רזא

ך"מנצפ ועם אתוון ב"בך נתונה הקדושה שתורתנו הידוע מן הקדושות שהאותיות לדעת וצריך. שבעתיים ומזוקקים זך הם טעם בכתיבתם נמצא שלא האומות כתיבת כפי הסכמיות אינן ואות אות כל, תורתנו אותיות אבל האות ותכונת למהות לאומרם אשר קץ ואין סוף אין עולמות לכמה בתכונתה מרמזת דרך ואות אות כל על לנדבר רק, כח בנו אין ולברורם אפשר אי ונתחיל. תכונתה מרמזת עולם איזה ועל שורשה מה כללית והוא ה"הקב זה "אלף" בדרושים מצאנו 'א האות סוד '. א באות ה"הקב כך, האותיות ראש שהאלף כשם, אחרון והוא ראשון כתיב הלא, האלף בתכונות ה"הקב נרמז איך ונאמר, לכל ראש אבל יתברך "לו תערכו דמות מה"ו "תמונה כל ראיתם לא כי" שמו היה עולמו את ה"הקב שברא שקודם להבין אתה צריך עולמות 'והד יתברך בעצמותו נעלם הכל והיה בגויה סתים נעלמים היו ה"ב ה'הוי שם אותיות 'ד נגד שהם ע"אבי בעצמותו 4 לציירם אפשר ואי ניכרים היו שלא עד בעצמותו כן ועל מחברו גבוה עולם וכל נעלמים שרשים בסוד רק יתברך האוזן לשבר רק לדבר אפשר שאי מה מחבירו גבוה שורשו ומכחם יתברך בעצמותו נעלמים גוונים 'ד בסוד בהם נדבר ותחתיהם עליהם שוכן ה"והקב עולמות 'הד ה"הקב ברא שלא העלמתם בעת שכן ומכל ע"אבי שיצאו לאחר אף ובינותם שאדם לנו וידוע. בתוכו נעלמים והם כלל ניכרים עדיין היו 'לד, הגוף [ללא] בלתי, שלו התוך שהוא הגוף נחלק החומרי מדרגות 'ב: מדרגה, הידיים עם הצוואר 'א: מדרגה: מדרגות מדרגה, הטבור עד הלב ב: מדרגה": שמעתי אחרת פעם) הלב המדרגה 'רגליים) 'הד המדרגה 'ובכלל ברית עד מטבור 'הג: צריך כן כמו. הברית עם הירכין 'הד, ומעיים הבטן חלק 'הג:

התוך כביכול ה"הקב שברא עולמות 'הד האוזן לשבר להבין עליהם כביכול והוא ע"אבי מדרגות 'לד נחלק והתוך שלו התוך כי הידוע מן. סוף ובלי קץ בלי עד ובסופם בראשם שברא שקודם נאמר, כן ואם משוך שהוא 'ו אות תכונת תכונתו התוך שעתה מה ג"הד בעצמותו נעלמים שהיו העולמות ה"הקב לזה יתברך בעצמותו נעלם מקודם והיה 'הו בתכונת ומרומז 'וי לעילא 'י: תכונתה 'א אות כי בתכונתה 'הא אות מרמזת כל ברא ה"שהקבה מרמז לעילא 'הי. באמצעיתא 'ו ואות לתתא כל בסוף הוא ה"שהקבה מרמז לתתא והיוד קץ אין עד העולמות שהיה להתוך מרמז באמצעיתא 'ו והאות סוף אין עד העולמות 'ד בסוד בגוויה סתים שמיה שהיה בעצמותו יתברך נעלם ושרשי יתברך ה'הוי השם שרשי הנקראים נעלמים גוונים 'ד הם בהתוך למה לך תקשה ואם: הגהה. עולמות 'הד שרשים ששה מספר שהוא 'ו בתכונת ומרומז עולמות 'ד סוד מדרגות שש הוא באמת כי דע? עולמות 'ו מדרגות 'ו להיות וראוי למטה מה למעלה מה לשאול אסור אבל קצוות 'ו סוד מדרגות את לברוא הפשוט ברצונו עלה וכאשר. באריכות הכל ויבואר

ולא עם בלא מלך אין כי, יתברך אלהותו לאשמודע העולם ומה העבד מוכנע בערכו האדון גדולת ולפי, עבדים בלתי אדון לפני מוכנע יותר הוא אדונו וממשלת גדולת יותר מכיר שהעבד הנעלמים גוונין 'הד שיצאו ברצונו עלה זה מטעם אשר אדוניו לברוא כדי והגס העב החומרי לגדר שיבוא עד ע"אבי כגדר אדונו גדולת ויבין פחיתתו שיראה כדי המדרגה בשפל האדם כדי "וגו שמיך אראה כי" כאמור ידיו ומעשה ממשלתו ורוב מטעם. ורעד בפחד לבוראו ויעבוד יתברך לפניו האדם שיוכנע נתן ולא ע"אבי גדר לידי ויבואו שיצאו ברצונו יתברך עלה זה היד שבודואי ל"הנ מטעם כביכול וביה מניה וקיום העמדה להם אחד בגדר עבדיו עם האדון משל דרך יהיה אלא? תקצר 'ה העבד אלא, העבד מגדולת ניכרת האדון גדולת אין אחד בחדר לגדר שיצאו צריך כן על, האדון ממחיצת חוץ להיות צריך

שעשוע יתברך לפניו היה הטוב ברצונו כך עלה וכאשר ע"אבי כי הפעולה כח במח מעורר הרצון באדם משל ודרך וחשק של הראש האוזן לשבירת כביכול המח מן בא הזרע כי , המולד אחד ניצוץ ממנו מתעורר היה , עילאה לנהורא מכנים אנו 'הא בהתוך הגליפו סוד יפעול ניצוץ ואותו 'הא של התוך לתוך וירד מהשרשים שיגלוף היינו ע"אבי גדר לידי שיבוא כדי יתברך היינו פועל לידי השם ויבוא הנעלם ה'הוי שם שורש הנעלמים אור שיגלוף אחר בו לבנות בהתוך הגליפה אחר שיפעל תחילה ונדבר. מכונו על עולם כל העולמות גדר המובחר כח לידי הנעלם השורש מן שבא הקדוש השם של מהגליפה שהיא יוד אות עד האותיות תכנוניות יובנו דברינו ועם ופועל ע"אבי מהעולמות נדבר כ"ואח הקדוש מהשם ראשונה אות
5. עילאה נהורא בכח הקדוש השם פעולת י"ע גדר לידי שיצאו מעולם הנעלם שורש היינו ,הלב גוון לתוך הניצוץ שירד דע להשורש יורד היה השניה מדרגה שאם שורש שהוא הבריאה לשורשו חוזר היה 'הא מדרגה שהוא מאצילות הנעלם , יחזור שלא מעכב 'הא והמדרגה 'הב למדרגה יורד כן על או 'הג ולמדרגה . שיבואר והבטישה התלהבות מכח לשרשו 'הד אבל, לסבלו כח להם שלא היה יהיה שלא לירד לו אפשר היה לא הניצוץ אור מכח התלהבות היה שם שגם אף 'הב במדרגה לידי לבוא שיכול קצת העמדה לו היה מכל מקום והנורא הגדול ומכח כנודע המח קצת בערך הוא שהלב כאשר פעולה שנבאר. כמו גליפה לידי בא זה שמכח הפעולה יהיה התלהבות שביציאת 'ב דאות רזא הוא הניצוץ ירידת והנה 'ב האות סוד פתח פתיחת בשכלך לצייר אתה צריך האוזן בשבירת הניצוץ פתח פתיחת ותצייר האלף ראש נקודת תכתוב ואם ליציאתו והדברות 'ב באות התורה מתחלת זה מטעם 'הב אות ציור הוא מי על "אלהיך 'ד אנכי"ב התורה תתחיל שאם "א"ב מתחילות תחילת שהיא 'בב מתחילה [התורה] אבל? הדיבור נופל יהיה אלהיך ה' אנכי דיבור נופל ועתה, לאשתמודע שברא הבריאה

לתוך הניצוץ ירד כאשר לדעת וצריך ג' האות סוד ת"ה.הבי אל אם אזניך למשל והטה ניצוצין תרין ממנו התנוצצו, הלב גוון לצדדים ניצוצות ממנה יתנוצצו, דבר על בוערת גחלת תיפול התנוצצו מהניצוץ כביכול כן כמו, חסירה אינה הגחלת וגוף ניצוצין התרין נקראו הגדול הניצוץ שבערך ניקודין תרין ב"כח דשרשי רזא והם לשמאלו 'וא לימינו 'א "ניקודין תרין" בעצמותו טמירתא נקודה בסוד והם כנודע כאחד ששקולין והתרין הגדול הניצוץ הוא הראש ג כזה ג' דאות רזא והוא סוד והוא ממנו שהתפשטו נקודות תרין הם הגימל של רגלין ו"ח וגבול ומידה אות בשום תהרהר ואל כאחד ששקולין ב"כח בגוון הנקודין עם הניצוץ שהתפשט וכיון. השרשים שרשי רק הוא הניצוץ שאור לפי גדולה בהתלהבות היה וביה מניה הלב כח לבקש הלב בגוון התעוררות והיה גדול יותר והוא המח אור לעלות הניצוץ מתעורר היה הגוון של התעוררותו ומכח לסבול שיחזור כח לו שבא [סברא שהיתה] סבר שהיה, למעלה לא באמת אבל, הניקודין עם להניצוץ מתעורר והיה למעלה שעולם היינו] לעיל שהתבאר כמו לעלות באפשר היה שיסבור יתברך הבורא ברצון והיה [לעלות ממנו מנע האצילות לבטשם נקודין התרין בהתעורותו שיעורר כדי לעלות הניצוץ העליון הניצוץ בכח מהם יצא שלהם הבטישה ומכח בזה זה בלי רסים ניצוצין לכמה התנוצץ 'הב ניצוץ ואותו אחר ניצוץ התנוצצו] התנוצץ מהניצוץ למה לשאול תרצה ואם. וקץ ערך דצריך? רבים ניצוצות התנוצצו 'הב ומהניצוץ נקודין תרין תרין התנוצצו כן על בנחת ירד העליון שהניצוץ להבין אתה לעלות הניצוץ התעוררות מכח ',הב ניצוץ אבל, ניצוצין מהם יצא בזה זה שבטשו הבטישה מכח , הניקודין והתעוררות רבים ניצוצות התנוצצו הכי משום, בסוד יורה כחץ בכח ניצוץ רזא הוא 'הב הניצוץ זה והנה 'ד האות סוד. וקץ שיעור בלי הניקודים של הבטישה מכח יצא 'הב הניצוץ כי 'ד דאות הניצוץ כן ואם העליון הניצוץ מהתעוררות היה והתעוררותם

התערותם מכח עתה 'ג דאות ברזא שהיו הניקודים עם העליון מהם ונעשה הנקודים בין הניצוץ שהתפשט היינו יחד 6 הזדווגו השני הניצוץ התפשט כך ואחר כזה 'ד אות של הרוחב קו ונעשה האורך וקו 'הד רגל והוא הימיני מצד היתה וההתפשטות היינו במקומם ויבוארו הקדוש משם הם 'ו ואות 'ה ואות 'ד אות 'ט 'ח 'ז אותיות סוד. מהשם ראשונה אות שהיא 'י אות אחר להיות שהתחיל שכיוון לדעת וצריך 'ז. אות עתה ונבאר כביכול והתגלגלו כביכול החימום נולד הלב בגוון התלהבות הניצוץ נגד להתאמץ סיבה מבקשים שהיו התוך כל של כח לדחוק הלב לגוון כחם בכל התאמצו למקומו להחזירו העליון ל"כן לפעול אפשרי להם היה לא זה באמת אבל למעלה האור. יתעורר זה ומכח הגוונים כל שיתעוררו הבורא רצון זה והיה ניצוצים שהתנוצץ הראשון הניצוץ ועם הנקודין עם הניצוץ להיות שלהבת כמו אסיפה סוד מהם נעשה ובהתערותם רבים בסוד העליון לניצוץ כח בו התפשט כ"ואח אחד ניצוץ כמו הניצוץ וכח שייפין בסוד הם שנאספו הרבים הניצוצין כי נשמה והתאמצו הגוון שהתעוררו ומכח כביכול נשמה בסוד העליון העליון הניצוץ ונטלה ששאבה הפעולה היתה זו כוחם בכל לשאוב עתה והתחיל התוך של המובחר כח הניצוצין שבתוך ולחקוק לשאוב שהתחילה וכיון והחקיקה הגליפה אותה מתוך עד הגוונים כח כל ולחקוק לשאוב מחשבה כח עתה נולד שיבואו ש"וב ה"ב ה'הוי שם שרשי כל ויחקוק שישאב ותשכיל תראה לך שכל עיני ואם ופועל כח לידי השרשים ירד שבתחילה "וגו אלוה אחזה מבשרי כי" הפסוק ותבין כ"ואח המוליד וכח הרצון והיה הלב גוון לתוך ונחת הניצוץ כח יורה בסוד רבים לניצוצים התנוצץ הלב התלהבות מכח בהם התפשט כ"ואח השייפין סוד אסיפה בסוד נעשה כ"ואח המחשבה סוד נולד הנשמה כח ומכח הניצוץ כח הנשמה כח היא הזאת והמחשבה, המחשבה סוד הוא הנשמה, כנודע ולחקוק לגלוף מחשב שהיה הקדומים לכל קדומה המחשבה

ופועל כח לידי כה שיבואו הנעלמים הגוונין ומתוך ה"הוי שרשי שפעלה אחר היינו סתם קדומה ממחשבה נדבר כ"ואח כח לידי ה"הוי שרשי שבאו, הקדומים לכל הקדומה המחשבה הפעולות לכל קדומה והיא הקדומה המחשבה כח נולד, ופועל ועתה ה"ב"ע יבואר כאשר העולמות בבנין הקדוש השם שפעל הרבים הניצוצים שנתאספו ממה ט"זח אותיות תכונות יובנו בסוד לו והוא המחשבה סוד בו ונולד ז אות ראש אחד בניצוץ והנשמה הזין של והעמדה רגל בסוד הוא והעמדה קיום מחלק וכשנאתה 'לב נ"הזי הרגל מחלק במחשבה בו שנתפשטה כי ח כזה ח"ה אות מהזיין נעשה באורך חלקים 'לב הזין רגל וכדי מחשבה פנימיות והנשמה לנשמה מלבישה המחשבה ת"החי רגלי נמשכו הנשמה כח לסבול למחשבה אפשר שיהיה 'הח על שלמעלה והגג הנשמה מדרגות 'ה בסוד ונתעבו לזה זה אפשר ויהיה לשרשה פתוח פתח לנשמה שיהיה כדי מעט נחלק סוד 7. טוהובן כזה 'ט אות ל"כנ ח"ה מאות נעשה כ"וא לסובלה 'ד כל ונבאר ד"יו אות תכונת לבאר נתחיל עתה 'ו 'ה 'י אותיות לנפשך מרגוע ותמצא בו כפול 'ה ולמה הקדוש השם אותיות. הקדומים לכל הקדומה המחשבה לסוד ל"הן לענין ונחזור מתוך ה'הוי שרשי ולחקוק לגלוף מחשב שהיה (ה"המקל להלן) לבקש חשב והנה. ופועל כח לידי שיבואו הנעלמים גוונין 'הד אורו ויחקוק ישאב ז"שעי כדי כחו ויגלגל התוך שיתאמץ סיבה הגדול הניצוץ אור שהסתיר ה"המקל פעל ויותר יותר במובחר האור שהעמיד עד הסתירה בסוד למעלה הנזכרים הניצוצים עם שכבר התוך שיחשוב בהסתירה והכוונה ד"יו של קוצו בסוד שהתאמצו במה שפעלו הואיל ויחשבו למעלה האור חזר כמו רק נשאר שלא עד ולמעלה האור מן שחזר עד בתחילה ולהתאמץ הלב לגוון כחם לעורר יחזרו זה מכח ד"יו של קוצו הרגיש לא והתוך שהיו כמו להיות למעלה הכל לחזור כדי בכח אור רק מחשבה בו שאין אור הוא ל"התוך שהסתירה בסוד ממה יותר האור התפשט מיד ל"הן התוך שהתאמץ וכיוון פשוט

87

כביכול אורו לתוך נגדו שהתאמץ החכ האור וחקק ושאב שהיה
כ"ואח ד"יו של קוצו בסוד האור הסתיר בתחילה ונמצא
היתה האור שהסתיר שהסתירה וכיוון ד"היו תוך בסוד התפשט
כתר בסוד הוא הקוץ לפיכך כ"אח יותר שיתפשט כדי הפעולה
בהתפשטות היה לא הקוץ היה לולי כי חכמה בסוד ד"היו ותוך
התחתון קוץ בסוד מאוד גבוה אור ממנה היוד תוך הורד כ"אח
קוץ בסוד למטה שהורייד האור כ"ג שהסתיר היינו ד"היו של
התוך שיסבור הטעם שאמרנו שלמעלה, ל"הנ מטעם לא אבל
להם עלתה ולא ל"הנ סברו כבר עתה אבל למעלה חזר שהאור
שבטלו התוך שסבר התחתון בקוץ הסתירה שהיתה רק
וכיוון שאבדו כוחם להם ויחזור לסבול שיוכלו בערך כשיעור
יותר האור התפשט התחתון מקוץ כוחם לבקש שהתאמצו
שלימה יוד נעשה התחתון והקוץ והתוך העליון והקוץ שהאור
לפי, עשר מספר והוא אחת נקודה הוא ד"היו ולפיכך י כזה
וכל קווין 'ג בסוד היו שלימה ד"יו לעשות שהתפשטו שקודם
בסוד בזה זה התפשטו כ"ואח 'ט הרי סוף תוך ראש לו יש קו
התפשטות בכל גדול כלל זה כי עשרה הרי ל"כן שלימה ד"יו
שהיה ונמצא במקומו העליון מן הרשימו נשאר האור שיתפשט
באותיות הקטנה שהיא יוד אות בתכונת האור העמדת תחילת
כדי שנבאר כמו קטנה אות נגד להתאמץ התוך יסבר זה שמכח
מכח הנעלמים השרשים ושאיבת הגליפו פעולת שתוגמר
כח התחיל ל"כן יוד כתכונת האור שעמד אחר. הבטישה
באור לנגוע להם שאפשר מה צד לבחון הנעלמים השרשים
בכחם והגבירו מהם הנאבד הכח להם [ולהחזיר] לחזור הגדול
וכחם, למקיף עליהם היוד שעשו היינו, היוד לתוך והעמידו
התוך כי [ונוקבא דכר] נ"דו חיבוק בסוד המקיף לתוך העמידו
הוא היוד שהוא והמקיף התוך שהוליד [נוקבא] ק"נו סוד הוא
הואיל וסברו. הכח לשאוב האור התפשט ולא, הדכר סוד
אור על להתגבר שיוכלו סברו היוד בתוך העמדה להם שמצאו
והמשיכו להתגבר יותר והתאמצו שאבדו הכח להם ויוחזר היוד

על העמידו המקיף בתוך שעמד ביושר לאורך המקיף קו וגבר הניצוץ אור התפשט כן שעמדו וכיון עליו לגבור כדי הקו של הקו בתוך כחם ונתמתק הקו אור לתוך הכח ושאב כחם על למקיף עליהם הקו עשאו שבתחילה מה עתה ותמצא. היוד השם מן ראשונה ה' אות נעשתה הקו לתוך כחם והעמידו עילאה אימא בסוד ראשונה ה' ולפיכך נ"ד חיבוק בסוד והיתה לבחון התחיל ששם באשר דינין מתערין הבינה ומן. בינה בסוד להם עלתה שלא פ"אע שהיו לכמו לחזור לנגוע שיוכלו מה צד ומה. בחינתם לבחון התחילו מקום מכל, כ"אח שהשתמתקו לפי נתמתק ששם ולפי ו' סוד הוא הקו על הכח כ"אח שהעמידו הכל הממתק הוא הקדוש משם ו' אות לפיכך הקו לתוך כחם להם עלתה לא זה שגם וכיון. המידה קו והוא 8 הכל והממזג חשבו לא מידם נאבד ן"דו חיבוק בסוד נגיעה להם שהיה ממה נמתקו כבר כי יותר להתגבר להם אפשר אי וגם להתגבר יותר העמדה להם להיות רק וחשבו השרשים המובחר כל 'הו לתוך עליהם מקיף ו' מאות לעשות וחזרו חיבוק בסוד בתחילה כמו. ותמצא אחיזה להם יש ושם ה'הוי של אחרונה ה' אות וזהו שכבר באשר כח לידי ש"וב ה"ב ה'הוי אותיות [שבאון] שבא תרצה ואם. העליון הניצוץ בכח הנעלמים שרשי כח כל בירר לא ראשונה 'ובה ההעמדה נשאר אחרונה ה' באות למה לשאול דלא ריעין בסוד הם ה"י אותיות כי לדעת לך צריך? נשאר האור. לסבול אפשר היה ולא הפסק בלא הזיווג ושם מתפרשין והוא יוד בתכונו הוא הדכר שם כי הפסק בלי הוא ששם והטעם מן ונעשה חזר לפיכך והפסקה מעצור בלי כביכול קטנה אות קו על מרמז יותר באורך שהוא ו' הוא הדכר סוד ועתה ה"ו ה"י לסבול שאפשר בכדי במידה ליתן ומפסיק מעציר והוא המידה. הכח שאב שכבר קדומים לכל הקדומה מחשבת נשלמה ועתה ממש 'הוי אותיות לפועל הקדוש השם בא כ"ואה 'הוי שרשי שרשים כח עתה שנברר רק ו"ח אות תמונת בשום תהרהר ואל להם נשמה כמו אחד אור והניצוץ כביכול שנעשה הנעלמים

האורות כל התפשטו ועתה הטוב כרצונו לפעול יכול ומעתה ועתה. למעלה רשימה בסוד ונשארו 'הוי אור לתוך שהזכרנו כדי הקדוש השם שפעל הפעולות לכל קדומה ממחשבה נדבר ברצון שעלה כמו וגבול גדר לידי שיבואו העולמות לברוא כח יתערב שלא וחשב הדברים בתחילת שהזכרנו כמו: הבורא הימני כח והוא נברר המובחר כי, הפסולת היינו הנשאר הגוונין זה לומר אפשר שאי פ"אע נשאר שלהם השמאלי וכח שלהם ימין לומר יתכן הבקיעה שלאחר הואיל אבל שמאל וזה ימין הימני כח והוא המובחר כח כאן השאלה דרך נאמר ושמאל גילגל כביכול הנברר באור הפסולת יתערב שלא וחשב שלהם כחומה יתברך סביב גלגל האורות מכל הנזכרות הרשימות מאור והרשימה הנשאר האור ובין הנברר האור בין המפסקת הקרוב משל דרך על. יותר קרוב מסבבת יותר הגבוה כ"ואח, עליונה נקודה אור מניצוץ הרשימו הוא אליו יותר מנקודה כ"ואח, שניה מנקודה כ"ואח, ראשונה מנקודה רשימה ה"קל ממחשבה כ"ואח, הנשמות לכל מנשמה כ"ואח, רביעית מקוץ]כ"ואח[, יוד של מתוך]כ"ואח[, ד"יו של מקוצו כ"ואח]כ"ואח[ה' מגוף כ"ואח, השלימה מיוד]כ"ואח[, התחתון כ"אח ה', מנקודות מגוף ו', מראש ו', מגוף]כ"ואח[ה' מנקודת ומה 'מי: לפועל שיצאה 'מהוי כ"אח, קדומה ממחשבה. אחיזה להם יש ושם בחיצונה המסבב היה אחרונה 'ומה מיניה ל"הנ הרשימות בתוך עצמו המסתיר העליון והניצוץ היה לא יתברך סביבות שנתגלגלו והרשימות הלב בגוון וביה 'הוי ואור כלל גוון ולא סומק ולא אוכם ולא חיור לא בהם ניכר ניכר שהיה עד הבהירות בתכלית מאיר היה בתוכם שנעלם אי ואילך לטושה מראה נוטל אדם אם, משל דרך. בהם להנות אפשר וקיום העמדה לו יתן אם אבל אורו להנכר אפשר כביכול היו לא והבטישה התלהבות מכח כביכול כן כמו, מאורו אורו ניכר ועתה להנכר אפשר היה ולא וקיום העמדה לאור. והבן וקיום העמדה לכלל שבא לפי הרשימות בתוך הגדול

לסבול אפשרי להם שיהיה העולמות פעולת שיתחיל כדי והנה, בזוהר הנאמר "בקע ולא בקע" סוד וזה לשנים העיגול ונבקע לחיצוניות חוץ הפנימי אור שהלך ההולדה סוד היא והבקיעה תבין האוזן ולשבר. החיצוניות מתוך הפנימיות שנגלף הגוונים מתוך האפרוח ונגלף הביצה פנימיות מתוך האפרוח מהולדת העיגול אור כל יצא שלא ודע. לשנים הביצה ונבקעה פנימיות אור בסוד שם נשאר השני והחצי החצי רק החיצוניות מתוך רק החיצוניות לתוך כולו הלך דהיינו אור ה'הוי' והגנוז הצפון 9 ומן הנשאר השני החצי תוך יתברך ממנו רשימה נשארה והחצי הימיני עימו ה'הוי' אור לקח העיגולים שבתוך הרשימה לומר שייכות אין הבקיעה שקודם פ"ואע שם נשאר השמאלי שהוא לפי למעלה שכתבנו כמו כן לומר יתכן מ"מ ושמאל ימין החצי הגוונים החיצוניות תוך שנשאר והטעם המובחר כח כביכול הצפון סבלות לידי האור שיבוא כדי חדא: השמאלי אור כל יוצאים [היו] אילו כי ועוד הצפון אור והוא מאורו הגוונים לחיצוניות היה לא הגוונים לחיצוניות מחוץ הרשימות אור אחר שירדפו בהכרח והיה וכלל כלל והעמדה קיום נשאר לפיכך, שהיה לכמו ו"ח חוזר והיה שלהם הפנימיות ש"וב ה"ב ה'הוי' מאור הרשימו נשאר וגם הרשימו של החצי שבנה העולמות שראו עד האור ביציאת כך כל הרגישו ולא התחילו כ"אח מהם שיצא הימיני הפנימי אור באותו הבורא לכמו לחזור לנגוע יוכלו שלא הבורא פעל כבר אבל לרדוף וכאשר. כנודע השבירה במקום אחיזה להם שמצאו רק שהיה עימו והלך הגוונים חיצוניות מתוך הימיני הרשימות החצי הלך ואור ההתפשטות בתכלית הימיני החצי והתפשט ה'הוי' אור היה ואז גבם על לעמוד הרשימות פנימיות מתוך הלך ה'הוי' ולאין סוף לאין הימיני הרשימות חצי של האור התפשטות גבי על כביכול לעמוד הלך ה"ב ה'הוי' שאור מטעם תכלית משורשו קיבל וכביכול ע"נ לשורשו ממש סמוך הרשימות שמצינו כ"א אור והוא תכלית ואין ס"ל לא האור להתפשט

ולפיכך הכל המכסה המלבוש בסוף והוא הראשונים בדברי כל מכסה שהוא לפי ס"א בסוד הוא דאצילות תפארת מידת הרשימות ג"ע ה'ההוי אור שהלך והטעם כנודע הספירות לסבול אפשר שיהיה כדי חדל לעיל שכתבנו טעמים מהשני חומרי גדר לידי שם לבוא אפשר שיהיה הרשימה תוך האור לשורשו חוזר המובחר שהאור הגוונים החיצונים שיסברו ועוד מהם שיצא הרשימה לחצי יהיה לא כ"ו א שהיה כמו לגמרי, הימיני החצי אחר ירדפו ולא להם שנשאר מהחצי כח יותר ואדרבא הרשימות ג"ע רק לגמרי לשורשו חזר לא באמת אבל שיצמצמו הצימצום אחרי העולמות שיבנו פעולה היתה זו קדמון אדם בסוד יהיה בצמצום נשאר והאור כביכול האורות תוך ה'ההוי אור נשאר היה ואילו. כנודע הקדומים לכל "וחי האדם יראני לא כי" בסוד לסבול אפשר היה לא הרשימות חזר לא אבל גבם על למעלה אורו הסתיר לפיכך (כ,לג שמות) אחר. ש"ו ב ה"ב ה'ההוי לכלל בא שכבר לפי לשורשו לגמרי נעשה ל"כן תכלית ולאין ס"לא הרשימות על האור שהתפשט שנראה עד הרשימות תוך הצמצום סוד היינו התנועה סוד בערך האור נשאר רק ו"ח מכל פנוי ולא פנוי חלל בתוכם לידי העולמות יבואו ידו שעל שהזכרנו ק"א אור והוא הסבלו האוזן לשבר נאמר ועתה. העליון הבורא ברצון בכח פועל וגבול מידה בשום תהרהר ואל ספיראן דעשר השרשים שרשי ש"ו ב ה"ב ה'ההוי אור ג"ע הכתר בסוד הוא עילאה נהורא. ו"ח והוא העולמות לכל הראש בסוד החכמה בסוד ה"ב ה'ההוי ואור הרשימות היינו, הימיני הגוונין ופנימיות דבר לכל קדמון בסוד והם ה'ההוי של שעשוע בסוד אימא בסוד הם, שהזכרנו יתברך ה'ההוי מן שהתפשט ס"א ואור עילאה נקודה ובסוד בינה ומכוסים תכלית ולאין ס"לא שהתפשט עד הרשימות לתוך ואור. לעיל שהזכרנו וטעם תפארת בסוד הוא ס"א אור באותו הקדמון בערך והוא קדמון אדם סוד הוא הצמצום תוך הנשאר על נופל אדם ששם ק"א אותו מכנים אנו ולפיכך היסוד בערך

וצדיק" ש"כמ העשיה עולם של היסוד הוא תחתון שאדם יסוד ה"הקב של היסוד כביכול שהוא ולפי (כה,י משלי) "עולם יסוד וצדיק" ש"כמ העשיה עולם של היסוד הוא תחתון שאדם יסוד ה"הקב של היסוד כביכול שהוא ולפי (כה,י משלי) "עולם יסוד שהיה ומה. קדמון נקרא ה"הקב כי "קדמון אדם" נקרא לפיכך ונקוט. יסוד ג"ע עטרה בסוד הוא החלל סביבות האור מתאמץ בתחילה שהיה הבקיעה קודם לעיל שאמרנו מה בידך כללא וחקיק גלוף בסוד בכח הלב בגוון וביה מיניה האור מתפשט, בא הגדול הניצוץ ואור בפועל הכל נעשה הבקיעה אחר עכשיו בסוד חכמה ובסוד העולמות לכל הראש בסוד ה'הוי לכלל עתה והתרין גבו 11 על כתר עילאה ונהורא. דבר לכל קדמון אבל א"או שורש שהם לומר שאפשר לעיל שאמרנו ניקודין אימא סוד הוא הימיני [והנקודה] והנקודות אבא הוא ה'הוי כאן מפנימיות הרשימות כל של הבית סוד עילאה בינה בסוד שהתנוצץ לעיל שכתבנו השני והניצוץ. הימיני מאור הגוונים האור סוד הוא הבקיעה אחר עתה ומהנקודין העליון מהניצוץ בסוד הכל לכסות תכלית ואין ס"לא יתברך ממנו שמתפשט ומה. הכל המכסה הרוח בסוד תפארת בסוד והוא המלבוש סוד הצמצום סוד הוא עתה הוא ניצוצות רבים בסוד לעיל שכתבנו ומה הנשמות לכל נשמה מסוד לעיל שכתבנו ומה התנועה חשב המחשבה והוא קדמוני לכל קדומה מחשבה מסוד שכתבנו זאת ולסיבה הנעלים ה'הוי של הרשימות בה ולחקוק לשאוב בסוד הוא עתה. ל"כנ יוד של קוצו בסוד האור והסתיר הקטין ק"א של האור כביכול והקטין קדמון אדם מלכות שהוא העטרה ה'הוי של עולמות 'הד שיבנה כדי כנודע יוד של קוצו בסוד ועתה. ה"בע שיבואר כמו ק"דא רגלוהי בין ס"א בכח בפועל כל כי, חוץ מחשבת בשום ו"ח תהרהר ואל ל"הנ שרשים תבין פשוט אור והכל האוזן לשבר רק הוא הנה עד שאמרנו מה אפשר היה לא ק"דא מלכות עד ס"א מאור והנה. גמור באחדות דרך, מעלה של האור התנגדות והוא בפועל העולמות להיות כח אלא ואינו כערכו אור אצלו ונורא גדול אור יש אם משל ק"דא מלכות עד ס"א מאור כן כמו, בשמו ונקרא הגדול האור

לפי הוא והענין. מעלה של קדמון אור הגדול האור כח הם נעלמים גווונין ד' בסוד יתברך בעצמותו נעלם האור שהיה מיניה שהיה קדמון אור מדרגות ד' לידי עתה האור בא, ל"כן בסוד ק"וא, מלבוש בסוד ס"א ואור ל"כן הרשימות עם וביה מיניה ונוקבא דכר בסוד והוא עטרה בסוד ק"דא ומלכות, יסוד רק להיות אפשר היה לא העולמות פעולת לכלל אבל. וביה שרוצה שמי ונודע. פועל לידי מתחילין ואילך ק"דא ממלכות

כן כמו היסוד על הבנין לעמוד יסוד לו צריך דבר לבנות רגלוהי מן עומדין דהעולמות, היסוד הוא קדמון אדם כביכול קו בסוד השפע יוצא רגליו ומבין. יתברך בחיקו דהיינו כנודע אורו לסבול העולמות שיוכלו כדי רק ע"אבי לעולמות היושר ע"אבי מדרגות ד'ל השפע שיתחלק מטעם וגם. והנורא הגדול רגלוהי בין פרסות ד' בסוד העולמות גבי על כביכול נעשה הרגליים ג"ע הפרסות על עומדים והעולמות יתברך בחיקו אחד וכל ע"ארמ יסודות ד' סוד הם והפרסות יתברך ק"א בחיק כי. ע"אבי לעולמות רישין תלת בסוד והם כנודע 'מד כליל חשבון בכלל ואינה ק"דא עטרה בסוד היא הראשונה פרסה כתר היא הרביעית פרסה כי, פרסות רישין שני רק אינן ובאמת בסוד והם שלימה קומה בסוד היא פרסה וכל דאצילות לפחות להתלבש לכהן שצריך הטעם וזה שמלבשים מלבושים נהורא בסוד גדול וכהן, כהן בסוד הוא ק"א כי. בגדים 'בד בגדים 'בח מתלבש הוא יתברך ממנו שיוצא והשפע, עילאה מקומו כאן אין בשמותיהם הבגדים 1 וטעמי. והבן כביכול שנתגלו ע"ארמ יסודות ד' בסוד שהם פרסות 'הד לענין ונחזור שורש לו ויש התחתון האדם ממנה שיבנה העשיה בעולם סוד בשורש הוא העפר כי "בצלמינו אדם נעשה" בסוד למעלה הוא שבאדם והמים עשייה שורש סוד והוא ק"דא המלכות הוא שבאדם ואש יצירה וסוד יסוד סוד ק"א סוד והוא הזיעה והרוח הבריאה וסוד הצמצום סוד התנועות סוד הוא החימום אצילות שורש וסוד ס"א ושורש ה'הוי שורש הוא שבאדם

שכל בכדי ל"הנ שרשים 'הד הגדול האור מלבישים והפרסות לנו תהיה ועתה לסובלו שיוכלו היינו פעולה לידי יבוא אחד ה"ב ע 'ת אות עד ואלף כף מאות האותיות להבין בנויה הקדמה מב שער חיים עץ: עיין וטעמם שמותם הכהן לבושי לבדבר 1 הפסח דרושי כ"שעה, פו-פה דפים חכם תורת, ב"מ א פרק למה לך יקשה ואם 11. ועוד תצוה 'פ המצוות טעמי, יב דרוש יהיו דברינו ולפי י"ט ח"ז ו"ה ד"ה ב"ג א: הם האותיות סדר אחר רמוזים ו"ה דברנו לפי כי זה כסדר שלא ל"הנ השרשים והיא שבאחדות אחרונה היא שהיוד התימה ויותר ל"כן היוד על הם שהאותיות לדעת לך צריך אבל. ה'הוי של ראשונה אות פ"אע האלף והנה. יתברך אחדותו על ומרמזים הספירות סדר ויו איוד כזה יוד הוא האלף וגוף יוד ותחתיו יוד גביו על שיש והיוד. כתר בסוד היוד של קוצו רק הוא מקום מכל דלת יתברך אחדותו על שניהם ומרמזים אחדים אותיות שבסוף חסדים גילוי בעצמותו שמגלה רק למטה הוא שלמעלה שמה ו"ה בהזדווגות כי, כנודע ו"ה באותיות שמרומזים וגבורות היוד הזיווג ובעת 'י בסוד והם תתאה 'בה עילאה 'ה מזדווג ישאר עדיין ואם. והבן 'לו קודם היוד לפיכך כביכול מתגברת בסוד ספירות היוד כי, דע.'לז 'ד בין הם ו"ה למה ספק לך סגולתא עליו יש: דעת היינו. כנודע סגולתא כעין הם מתקלא וגבורה חסד דעת סגולתא עליו יש: תפארת. ובינה חכמה כתר ובהזדווגות. ויסוד הוד נצח כביכול סגולתא עליה יש: מלכות משל דרך. יוד של קוצו סוד והוא הדעת נולד ובינה חכמה כתר אינו ואם, מפיו שיצא הדיבור ממנו נולד אזי מדבר אדם אם במחשבתו הדעת לו נולד אזי, מחשבתו חושב רק דבריו מדבר ומלכות תפארת בזיווג כביכול כן כמו. המוחין התגלגלות י"ע ב"כח ובהזדווגות בפועל מולידים הם אזי ודיבור קול בסוד הדעת סוד נולד כנודע יוד באות המרומזים המוחין סוד שהם 'הד ג"ע ב"כח של סגולתא הם ג"אב כן ואם. יוד של קוצו והוא בסוד אלא ניכר אינו אך קוצו בסוד הוא כתר כי. לדעת שמרמז

מה הזיווג וסוד האותיות שמשרשי אמרנו וכבר שבמוחין הדעת וזהו ג"חו ומזווג הכולל תפארת בסוד הוא הדעת בסוד שהיה במספר ז' ולפיכך י"לנה מרמזים ט"זח כ"ואח ל."כנ ו"דה כן וכמו תשעה ט' ושמונה ח' השביעית מידה הוא שנצח שבעה שהוא ל"הנ על מורה ד"יו כ"ואח מספרם לפי ו' ה' ד' ג' ב' לא ומתוך. אלו דברינו קוצר להבין היטב ודוק אחרון והוא ראשון ותפארת ג"דה ב"כח הם שאמרנו סגולתא בכל תבין דברינו ל"הנ פנימיות היא התפארת כי סגולתות בחשבון אינם ומלכות השייפין כביכול הם הסגולתא כי לספיראן נשמה כביכול והיא עשר" סוד הדעת בסוד נשמה הוא ותפארת האוזן לשבר עשר. יצירה בספר הנזכרים "עשרה אחד ולא עשר, תשע ולא תחלוק שלא, לתפארת דעת בין תחלוק שלא עשרה אחד ולא עצמה בפני מלכות ו"ח תחשוב ולא ומלכות תפארת בין ו"ח רק לבך על יעלה לא זה העשר לחשבון ו"ח יעלה ולא לקומה בחשבון והיה עטרה בסוד מלכות ולהיות שלים ביחודא ליחדו לבאור נבוא ועתה. כולם מיחד ה"ב ותפארת כביכול השייפין ואם, כתר תכונות על ציורה מורה כ' אות כ אות סוד כ' אות לתכונת מורה יותר ויהיה 12 כזה תכונתו לא למה תשאל קומת כי כ כזה באמת הוא בערכנו הכתר תכונת כי, דע? כתר קומת רק לשמים מארץ האדם קומת כמו אינה המרכבה כי, מאד רחב באור צריך וזה. לארץ שמים בין היא המרכבה הוא ולמעלה הכדור ומחצי אחד כדור הם וארץ השמים כדור זה בתוך זה הם העולמות וכל ארץ הוא השני והחצי שמים השני והחצי שמים הוא כדור החצי עולם ובכל בצלים כגלדי תתמה ואל לארץ שמים בין המרכז בנקודות בוקע והקו ארץ שתחתיו והחצי שמים הוא הקו גבי שעל החצי ולמה כן שאם לו יאיר כיום לילה" ה"ב י"הש שהרי בזה תתמה אל, ארץ הוא שמים יתברך ולפניו) יב,קלט תהלים פי על("כאורה וחשיכה יתברך שהשם רק ביניהם חילוק ואין אחד אור שניהם וארץ השני החצי מגשם היה אורו לסבול שיוכלו כדי ברחמיו ה"ב

והנה. ערכו לפי העולם כל לסבול שיוכלו בכדי הבריות בעיני
אין בתוכם אבל פרסות 'הד תוך ק"מא לבקוע היושר קו התחיל
ניכר להיות התחיל האצילות עולם לתוך שמגיע עד ניכר הקו
והיוד גבו על 'וי 'ו שהוא כזה ו בסוד נמשך והקו הראש בסוד
הארצי הכדור לחצי מביט שלה והפנים מגולה והוא הפנים הוא
מלובש והוא סביב הגוף הוא 'הו ומשך בריותיו על להשגיח
כל ממלא והוא מלובש הוא כולו העולם דהיינו ספירות בעשר
ברזא הספירות פנימיות הם ו'הוי ובמשך אורה העולם
והבן ובעיגול ביושר הם במלבוש אבל. סגולתא כעין דמתקלא
כל תוך זה דרך על הבוקע היושר קו אחר במקום ויבואר
כן וכמו ו בתכונות הוא באצילות דהיינו ע"אבי העולמות
אינו אבל לעשיה הקו בוקע היצירה ומן. ביצירה כ"וך בבריאה
של מקו עוקץ רק אינו שבעשיה הקו שכל רק ל"כן 'ו בתכונת
והקו כעוקץ רק הוא היצירה בערך העשיה גולם כל כי, יצירה
הוא ובעשייה. ביצירה עשייה מחבר לעשיה יצירה מן שנמשך
ל"כן מלובש והוא ל"כן האויר כל ממלא כ"וג מגושם קו
הולכים אם כ"וא. ודוק בוקע הקו אין ושוב סופו עד ונמשך
תחת היינו, השכינה כנפי תחת המרכבה רוחב תחת בקומה
שמחלק המרכז של דרך היא המרכבה קומת אבל, המלכות
כתר תכונת כן ואם, למערב ממזרח קצה אל מקצה וארץ שמים
באורה יבוא הפשוטה וך.. והבן ל"כן כ כתכונת הוא בערכינו
ל אות ל סוד ה."בע ד"מנצפ באותיות עצמו בפני באור
של ל"כן ווין תלת בסוד שהוא קו היושר סוד על תכונות הוא
יצירה של בעוקץ נכללת עשיה כי ויצירה בריאה אצילות
יכונה באצילות. ויוסף יעקב, ישראל: בסוד הם ווין והתלת
בבריאה יכונה "יעקב", הדעת בסוד שהוא "ישראל" בשם
בעשיה יצירה מחבר ועוקץ יסוד סוד שהוא ביצירה "יוסף"ו
הקדושה בתורתנו לזה מופלא ורמז. ומלכות יסוד חיבור שהוא
ויקרא כן כמו "שמות ואלה" 'בו שני ספר 'בב מתחלת בראשית
"הדברים אלה" 'בא הדברים ספר מתחיל כ"אח וידבר כן כמו

ה"אהי 'גימ א"בווו הם חומשין 'ה התחלת האותיות כל ובצרוף העיגול בקיעת של הימיני הכדור החצי דהיינו 'להב מרמז ומצד לאכסדרה דומה עולם סוד והוא באריכות כנזכר שנחלק בסוד 'הב תוך הבוקע לקו מרמזין ווין תלת. פתוח צפון 13 שהוא ומורה ס"א על מורה 'והא ל"וכנ יוסף יעקב ישראל הקו בתכונת הוא 'הל תכונת לעניו ונחזור. אחרון והוא ראשון האצילות לקו מרמז דקה שהיא הלמד גבי שעל ויו היושר במשך הרוחב בא שניה 'ו בבריאה כמו כך כל ניכר שאינו בא השלישי 'והו ניכר האור ששם הבריאה לקו מרמזת שהיא בוקע הקוץ כי ועשייה יצירה מרומזת זה שבקו לפי כקולמוס אינה עולמות לשני מרמזת שהיא ולפי לעשייה יצירה עולם מן פתוחה 'מ אות מ סוד. כקולמוס עגולה רק שווה במשך ועולם עולם כל והענין. למטה פתוחה והיא 'י 'ו 'כ צורת היא שבכל והקו ל"וכנ הקו בוקע ועולם עולם ובכל 'כ בסוד הוא הוא הקו הבריאה אחר ובאמת ל"וכנ ויוד ויו בסוד הוא עולם באותו לסבלו התחתונים שיוכלו כדי העולם בתוך מלובש סדר שמרמזים האותיות בסוד מדברים אנחנו העולמאבל ועל העולם חיות והוא לעולם קודם הוא הקו סדר ולפי הבריאה כדי למטה פתוחה שהיא ומה פתוחה 'מ אות תכונת זה סתומה ם מ אות סוד. שתחתיו לעולם מעולם הקו שימשוך המלבוש בסוד ל"וכנ הסתיר כביכול ה"ב שההויה לעיגול מרמזת ל"וכנ כו היא פתוחה ם"מ כי ה'ל'להוי מרמזת פתוחה ם"ומ והנפש העיגול בקיעת בסוד היא נון אות סוד. ה'הוי 'גימ אפשר היה לא בשווה שווה היה אם כי: כזה היא והבקיעה ימין שיגביר וכדי שווה ושמאל ימין היה כי העולם להתקיים העולמות ביסוד למטה להיות צריך התגברות ועיקר שמאל על צד של הקו משך עד היסוד כל הימיני ן"הנו למטה לפיכך פשוטה ונון כפופה נון הבקיעה מסוד שנעשה ונמצא שמאלי וילובש ימין בסוד הכל יהיה הקטרוג כשישתוק לבא ולעתיד העולם ויהיה סתומה ם"מ בסוד ויהיה הכפופה תוך פשוטה הנון

'ס אות 'ס אות סוד. אמן בימנו במהרה השלמות בתכלית שלם בסוד שהיה מה כביכול עצמו את ה"ב ס"ה א צמצום בסוד היא ואותו וביה מיניה לעולמות מקום המציא תכלית ואין ס"א שהוא לפי 'ס באות הצמצום מרומז ולפיכך סוף לו יש מקום ואות "סוף" מתיבת ראשונה אות והוא הסמך וגם הצמצום צורת קץ לאין העולמות בתוכו להוליד כביכול בטן בסוד היא 'ס אזנך עשה הנה 'ע אות 'צ 'פ 'ע אותיות סוד. מספר ולאין דבר הסתר אלקים סוד, בזה להאריך אפשר אי כי כאפרכסת "אלוה אחזה מבשרי" כי, דע. דבר מתוך דבר להבין וצריך וכבר הבטן סוד והוא ל"כנ ס"א באור צמצום שהיה כיון והנה 'לד נחלק שהגוף משל דרך דברנו בהתחלת לעיל אמרנו הברית חלק הוא 'הד וחלק הבטן חלק הוא 'הג וחלק מדרגות נשלם הגוף מחלק שלישית קומה כביכול היתה. וכאשר וירכין הקדמון בכח התעוררות בא להזדווג שצריך הגברא כח שצמצם ס"א והאור דכר סוד יוד בסוד והוא למטה שהתפשט [מתנועע] מתנוע והיה תנועות בסוד היה למעלה כביכול עצמו נ"וד חיבוק בסוד והוא העליון כח האור עם כביכול ומתרחק ואף דלתתא יוד בסוד הם והתנועות מתפרשין דלא ריעין בסוד עצמו התפשט העליון והכח למעלה עלה שהתנועות פי על הוא והכח שעשוע בערך רק אינם התנועות מ"מ כביכול למטה הוא באמצע והרי 'א אות של דלתתא יוד והתנועות דלעילא יוד עתה והנה. דברנו בתחילת שכתבנו 14 כמו הדכר של הגוף אות עד 'א מאות דיברנו עתה עד כי. מתכוננתה על 'ע אות תבין היה ולא הדכר כח כביכול הקומה רוב נשלם היה לא עדיין 'ס אלף בסוד הכל והיה לעולמות פעולות להוליד זיווג התעוררות 'ע 'א מן נעשה הצמצום אחר עתה אבל. ומכוסה א"פל אותיות כי. שעשוע להיות למעלה הלכו התנועות בסוד דלתתא היוד כי השעשוע בעת אלף באות דלתתא היוד רק 'א כצורת 'ע צורת וגוף עין צורה ונעשה דלעילא יוד בערך מתגברת היא והזיווג בפרסא ומכסה שוחה רק שהיא 'א באות כמו 'ו צורת הוא העין

הימיני היוד מצרף וכשאתה. עזר ע' ואות כביכול הזיווג לפני יוד ואות כפופה נון צורת היא העין גוף משך עם ע' אות של גוף משך עם ע' אות של הימיני שהיוד ומה נ"דו והוא בתוכו ומה נ"דו והוא בתוכו יוד ואות כפופה נון צורת היא העין לפי השנייה יוד בערך גבוה הוא האות העין הימיני שהיוד סוד היוד כ"ואעף עליו מתגברת היא בביאה הזיווג שבעת פ' ע' שאותיות ודע. ליוד סמוכה היא והנון למעלה הוא הדכר מתגבר והדכר נ"דו חיבוק שהיה כיון ל"ר פצע אותיות צ' רשימות כי פה בסוד והוא ק"דנו פצע נעשה כביכול זה ומכח פציעה בו נעשה התגברות ומכח החיבוק שלשלות הוא פא אות היא שהב"ש רק ל"כמש' נוק סוד כ"ג הוא ב' האות והנה פה בסוד רוב שנשלם עד הולדה כח היה שלא מוחין ובסוד בינה בסוד יהיה שלא כדי למטה המוחין מן היוד התפשט ועתה. הקומה אמה בסוד הולדה כח הוא הפא שבתוך והיוד בהתגלייא זיווג סוד והוא הפא סוד שהוא וכיוון הדכר בסוד ומתחבר 'נוק יסוד כביכול מתפשט היה, כלים כ"ואח משכן בסוד, המשכן ביעין תרין בסוד נ"דו יודין תרין בסוד מהמוחין מלמעלה הוא צ' ואות עולם יסוד צ' אות צורת והוא יסוד בסוד ונעשה אות צורת כי העולמים חי בסוד צ' אות עד אלף מאות י"ח אות ברוחב קצת נמשך הקו רק עין צורת היא זו וצורה כזה צ' הזיווג התעוררות על מורה הוא העין תכונת כי והענין. בפרסה בצ' השתנות היה ולא המוחין של היסוד הוא צ' ואות במוחין למה לך יקשה ואם. באתכסיא שיהיה כדי הפרסה משך רק כ"ואח משכן סוד שהוא הזכרנו כבר צ' לאות קודמת הפא ו"ח והיו הגבורות היו יסוד בסוד צ' בתחילה היה שאם, כלים ובזה, והבן בתחילה משכן נעשה כן על, לבטלה חסדים מים סוד ת"קרש אותיות באור אל נבוא ועתה. צ"עף אתוון תבין שהעולמות דבר לכל מקדמון ירכין תרין הוא ק' אות אור שנברר הגליפא בסוד למעלה בארנו וכבר עליהם עומדים בסוד נשארה הגוונין שהחיצוניות עד הגוונין מן המובחר וכח

אחיזה למצוא כח להם היה ולא סדין בסוד והם אחוריים שנעשה אחר ועתה הפנימי באור ולהתערב להתעורר שיוכלו טיפה בסוד הסדין על נשאר כביכול הקדוש הזיווג סוד חי בסוד בין אחיזה מצאו זה ומטעם. והתעוררו אחיזה ומצאו אחרונה עולם עד אחיזה לה יש זה ומטעם הזיווג מקום ירכין תרין קרקע כי, כנודע דאצילות מלכות עד לומר רצה, הבריאה וטיפה סדין בסוד היו והם אחרונה טפה בסוד היא דאצילות קרקע עד אחיזה להם יש לפיכך הסדין על נפלה אחרונה, ירכין התרין על עומדין הם ע"בי עולמות ג' כי, דאצילות להם יש ובירכין ע"בי העולמות של היסודות הם והירכין עולם אבל ע"בי עולמות בג' אחיזה להם יש לפיכך, אחיזה צורת תבין ובזה אחיזה להם אין ושם בטן בסוד הוא האצילות הרגל ומשך דאצילות קרקע על המקיף הקו משך ק אות השמאלי בירך שלהם אחיזה שעיקר ולפי החיצוניות על רומז, הודעתיך וכבר. שמאל לצד והיא אחת רגל 'ק לאות יש לפיכך ובעולם "ויט, ויבא 15, ויסע" של ווין בתלת מרמז היושר שקו אחיזה להם יש ממילא יצירה של עוקץ רק 'ו שם אין העשיה של השמאלי בצד רק ו"ח 'הו בגוף הכוונה ואין ווין בתרין הם ווין ותרין 'ר אות סוד. שלה בחיצוניות היוי של שעשוע 'ש אות סוד ר אות מורה ז"וע ש"ע ן"נו באות ל"כמש 'ר בסוד שהזדווגו מכח ווין תלת תכונת על צורתה מורה 'הש והנה אחרונה טיפה בסוד אחיזה להם בא זה מכח הקווין פנימיות סיבת ולפיכך ש באות שמרומזין הקדושות הטיפות רושם והוא שקר הוא אבל ווין לתלת כח להם שיש הסוברים החיצונים רק להם אין כי זה אחר זה עומדים שקר אתוון תלת ולפיכך של חותמו והיא 'ת אות כ"אח בא ז"וע 'ת אות סוד פסולת מות מילת כ"ג ומרמזת סוף תוך ראש "אמת" חותמו כי ה"הקב ל"כן מסתומה בסוד יהיה כי העולם מן יבוערו שהקליפות ל"ר ע ב ל ש ו ת. סליק

Printed in France by Amazon
Brétigny-sur-Orge, FR